# GONERS

## 1/ RU1:2

W9-AWD-018

*Other Avon Camelot Books in the*
**GONERS** *Series by*
*Jamie Simons and E.W. Scollon*

(#2) THE HUNT IS ON

*Coming Soon*

(#3) ALL HANDS ON DECK

Avon Books are available at special quantity discounts for bulk
purchases for sales promotions, premiums, fund raising or educa-
tional use. Special books, or book excerpts, can also be created to
fit specific needs.

For details write or telephone the office of the Director of Special
Markets, Avon Books, Dept. FP, 1350 Avenue of the Americas,
New York, New York 10019, 1-800-238-0658.

# 1/ RU1:2

**JAMIE SIMONS
and E.W. SCOLLON**

**Illustrations by MICHAEL EVANS**

AN AVON CAMELOT BOOK

This is a work of fiction. Names, characters, places and incidents either are the product of the author's imagination or are used fictitiously. Any resemblance to actual events, locales, organizations, or persons, living or dead, is entirely coincidental and beyond the intent of either the author or the publisher.

AVON BOOKS
A division of
The Hearst Corporation
1350 Avenue of the Americas
New York, New York 10019

Copyright © 1998 by Jamie S. Simons and E.W. Scollon, Jr.
Interior illustrations copyright © 1998 by Michael Evans
Interior illustrations by Michael Evans
Published by arrangement with the author
Visit our website at **http://www.AvonBooks.com**
Library of Congress Catalog Card Number: 97-94282
ISBN: 0-380-79729-1

All rights reserved, which includes the right to reproduce this book or portions thereof in any form whatsoever except as provided by the U.S. Copyright Law. For information address Writers House, Inc., 21 West 26th Street, New York, New York 10010.

First Avon Camelot Printing: March 1998

CAMELOT TRADEMARK REG. U.S. PAT. OFF. AND IN OTHER COUNTRIES, MARCA REGISTRADA, HECHO EN U.S.A.

Printed in the U.S.A.

OPM 10 9 8 7 6 5 4 3 2 1

If you purchased this book without a cover, you should be aware that this book is stolen property. It was reported as "unsold and destroyed" to the publisher, and neither the author nor the publisher has received any payment for this "stripped book."

For my favorite Earthlings:
Dhara, Hannah, Maeve, and Rebeccah.
—J.S.

For Justin, Alex, and Barbara,
for their love and support.
—E.W.S.

# ACKNOWLEDGMENTS

Special thanks to John Hennessy, Emily Hutta, and Lisa Sturz for their creativity; to Nancy Parent and Spencer Humphrey for help giving shape to the idea; to Amy Berkower and Fran Lebowitz for their guidance; to Stephanie Siegel for first falling in love with the project; and to Elise Howard, for being editor extraordinaire.

**1/ RU1:2**

# 1

## Rubidoux

Two days ago. That's when it all started. I was sitting in class. Planetoid Roma, Diplomatic Universal Headquarters. We call it "DUH." I don't mean to brag, but DUH is where all the smartest life forms in the universe are sent to become intergalactic diplomats.

Like most of the other kids, I've been at school on this chunk of rock since I was five. Scary, huh? Actually it's not all that bad. Being sent to DUH is the highest honor there is. There are 127 worlds in the Planetary Union. And it's the diplomats who hold it all together.

So what do we do at DUH? Study, study, study.

Bor-r-ring! Especially this class: Dead and Dying Worlds 101. If they are dead—over, gone, *done for*—why worry about them? The places I want to know about are the war-torn, hostile places. That's where all the cool stuff happens. You see, the Planetary Union, or PU, is worried about violence from these worlds spreading to us and infecting our peace. So the Union sends secret missions to these planets.

The top mission specialists get to mingle with the locals. They teach them about peace, then get out. If the planet eventually gets it, they are asked to join the Union. If peace is too hard a concept to wrap their minds around, we cut them off—forever. Now that's my idea of a cool job!

I was daydreaming about being on a mission to one of these planets, when suddenly I heard . . . "Roma to Rubidoux. Hello! Professor Toesis here. We're waiting for your answer."

Panicked, I came up with the only response that made sense. "Huh?"

"No, DUH, Mr. Doux. Remember? You're in class studying to become a guardian of our culture. A diplomat of peace. The hope of the Union. With your attention span I fear for the future, Mr. Doux."

"No, no, I'm with you."

"Then would you care to explain the meaning of the golden arches?"

*Ugh! Not Earth again. Who cares about the least known of the lesser planets?*

Glaring at me, the professor cleared his many throats. I stood up. But nothing came. Not one thought. I was breathing hard. My palms were sweating. Then, just as the professor started stomping down the aisle toward me—one breath from the sulfur-sucking Professor Hal E. Toesis and you are dead meat—a tentacle on my left lower lobe began to jiggle. Hallelujah! Saved!

"The golden arches were found on religious temples scattered all over Earth," I said, stopping Toesis in his tracks. "People would visit them three times a day to feed their souls by inhaling a thin, brown, rubbery disc covered by a red, sweet, sticky substance on a sesame seed bun."

"Very good, Mr. Doux. Perhaps there's hope for the Union yet. You may sit down."

I took my seat next to my best friend, Xela (she pronounces it Shay-la). She's the only thing that makes this very dead class bearable. Leaning over she whispered, "Pulled that one off by the skin of your tentacle."

I wiggled my antennae at her. "Thanks to you."

"You should be thanking the six stars of Erin you can read minds," Xela said with a laugh.

It's true that, like everyone from Douxwhop, I'm telepathic. Well . . . sometimes. At fourteen, I've got a long way to go before I'm great at it. But with

Toesis breathing down my neck, I'll take what I can get. Or what thoughts Xela's willing to send me.

"Actually, Xela, I'm going to thank them for making you a genius. So I don't have to be." That's one of the things I like about Xela. She's smart. Really smart. One look into her huge yellow pupils and you know there's more than air filling the space between her lobes. But she doesn't brag about it. She's cool.

Which is more than you can say about some of the life forms around here. Take the guy sitting in front of me. At least I think he's sitting. His name is She-Rak. And he looks like a tadpole with spiked hair. When he eats he chews up his food, then smears it on his skin so he can soak up the nutrients. Trust me, he's no one to take on a picnic.

Then there's Gogol. He's the weirdest specimen of all. Smooth skin. Straight hair. No scales. No antennae. I know not everyone in the universe can have the good looks of Douxwhopians—tall, bronze leathery skin, masses of braided, purple tentacles—but this is one sick-looking puppy.

*Just look at him,* I thought. *Hand's in the air. As always. Probably can't wait to correct something I said. And check out old Hal E. Toesis. He beams whenever Gogol speaks up.*

"Yes, Gogol?"

"To add a little something about the golden arches . . ."

4

Blah, blah, blah. I just had to tune him out. It was a matter of survival.

"Who let him into this school anyway?" I whispered to Xela.

"Come on, have a heart."

"No, thanks, I already have four."

"Very funny, Rubi. If you ask me, Gogol's not that bad. In fact, I kind of like him."

"Like him? He looks weird. He acts weird. He *is* weird."

"I don't know. I think he's kind of cute."

All at once, the professor's voice boomed, "Excuse me, are we interrupting you two?"

I gave him my most winning smile. "Not at all, Professor Toesis. We were just discussing . . . life forms. Earthling life forms . . . that's it, isn't it Xela?"

"Care to share your findings with the class?" asked the professor.

"Yes, Xela, care to share our findings?" I was hoping she'd come up with something. Anything. And she did.

"You owe me one," Xela whispered as she rose from her seat. "Professor Toesis, since Gogol seems to be the expert on dead worlds, perhaps he'd like to tell us what he knows."

A look of pure joy spread across Gogol's face. This guy was so sickening he made eating with She-Rak sound good. Naturally, he jumped up.

"While no actual pictures exist of what Earthlings looked like, our scientists believe that they took a variety of forms. Some walked upright on two feet. Some were furry and walked on four feet. Some flew."

"Excellent, Mr. Gogol. And now, Mr. Doux."

Thankfully, the hitsu chimed just in time. "Got to go, Professor Toesis. Can't be late for my next class." I vaulted over the furniture and grabbed Xela's arm as she headed for the door. "Xela, meet me after dinner at the usual place."

"I don't know, Rubi. All day long I've had this really bad feeling. Maybe we shouldn't . . ."

"Don't tell me you're scared!"

"I didn't say that."

"You don't need to," I said, wiggling my antennae.

"Rubi, do me a favor and put a hat on it."

I stared hard. Right into Xela's yellow eyes. "And you, do me a favor. Be there."

# 2

## Rubidoux

It was dark when I made my way to our meeting place. Pitch dark. The only light came from the slime in the ditch that runs along the outer wall of the school. It's filled with vile stuff that smells like burnt paste. Comes from the kitchen, of course. I'm used to it, though. I come here a lot. Enough to know that the only way to reach the mouth of our secret cave is to slog through ankle-deep muck. And to hold your nose.

The cave entrance is blocked by a heavy metal gate. It was bolted shut—as always. I got out my wrench and got busy. I could never believe how easy it was to get in here even with the gate locked tight. Anyone could do it! Guess not too many students wanted to risk getting caught and being expelled. But what's life without a little excitement? Four more bolts to go . . .

All at once, a cold, damp hand clamped onto my shoulder. I froze. My breath started coming in small little wheezes. My hearts were pounding. Another hand grabbed me. My career as a diplomat passed before my eyes. I began to make little gurgling sounds. Then a third hand wrapped around my neck. I relaxed. And turned around to face Arms Akimbo. "Not funny!"

Arms beamed from ear to ear. "Yes, it was."

Arms Akimbo. She's young, as you can tell from her idea of a practical joke. But she's also a genius. And one of the fastest thinking, fastest moving life forms on Roma. Arms attached herself to Xela the first year she got here. And now she's part of the gang. Which, when she's not using her four arms and twenty-four triple-jointed fingers to sneak up from behind and scare you to death, is a very good thing. All those arms and fingers can come in handy.

She put them to work now unscrewing bolts. But even as she worked, she kept looking around. "Hey Rubi, where's Xela?"

I didn't want to answer. But what could I do? "I don't think she's coming, Arms. It's just you and me. I'll understand if you want to leave."

Arms turned to look at me. Even in the dim light

**8**

I could see her color growing brighter, flushing her cheeks as she spoke. "Look, Rubi. Every night for three months we've been coming down here to map these tunnels. They are dark. Damp. Scary. Smelly. And weird. I could get caught. Sent home. Have my life ruined forever. Tonight is the night we go to the only section we've never seen. Maybe no one has ever seen. The slimiest, scariest, most remote part of The Tunnels. If you think I'm going to let you go there alone just because Xela backed out . . ."

I held my breath. Arms put her face right up to mine. "You're right."

She turned and started back through the muck. I got busy with the gate. So this was it. I was going in alone. Well, that's what diplomats do. They're brave. Daring. Bold. The last bolt fell free and the gate creaked open. I took a long look into the gloomy cave, then took a deep breath and entered.

The air felt clammy, cold. I was concentrating hard. Putting one foot in front of the other. I didn't want to go down in the slime.

Suddenly, I thought I heard a sound behind me. I stopped. Strained to hear. Nothing. I took another step and slipped! As I did, something grabbed me. And started tickling!

"Rubidoux," said Arms, "did you really think I'd let you go alone?"

I tried to grab her hands, but she jumped back

9

too fast. And if she'd jumped back, why was I still being tickled? I looked again. How could I have missed it? A dim, rainbow-colored light flickering off the walls of the cave. It came from a prism-like eye in the back of a head.

"Xela!" I cried. "You decided to come!"

Xela held up a light stick. "Only to talk you out of this. Look, Rubi, all day I've had a weird feeling. Something's just not right."

Arms looked at me. We'd learned long ago to trust Xela's feelings. She might not have antennae, but in some ways she could pick up things better than me. Now she had me worried. But we were so close. After three months. The best part of The Tunnels. Ours. Tonight. I winked at Arms.

"Oh, come on, Xela. This is Roma, the universe's most controlled planetoid. Nothing ever happens here. Nothing's going to happen tonight."

"I wouldn't want to bet on it," Xela said as she took the light and started moving toward The Tunnels. "But there's no way I'm letting you two go alone."

# 3

## Arms Akimbo

Xela kind of gave me a scare about going into The Tunnels. But I say, what's life without adventure? Classes. That's what. This is a lot more fun. Obviously Xela must have decided so, too. She'd already moved halfway down the cave, taking the light stick with her. Rubi and I had to run to catch up.

Xela reached the edge of the steep drop-off at the back of the cave and stopped dead. That's where the series of narrow ledges carved into the face of the underground cliff began. Ages ago we discovered that they led into the heart of Roma. Glowing phosphorus ooze from the river far below filled the cavern with an eerie light. Xela turned to face us.

The ghostly light made her look like a Phanta-morian.

"Arms, are you sure you want to go through with this?" she asked. She was so serious it made me kind of nervous. But I nodded yes. Rubi did too.

"Come on, Xela," Rubi said. "Let's get on with it."

"Fine. Don't say I didn't warn you," she said. Then she handed me the light stick. "There's no way I'm going first."

*Lucky me,* I thought. I started down, watching for the small shaft that cuts into the cliff at the halfway point. It's a tight squeeze, but it's the only way into the Crisscross. I named it that. It's a huge place where all the major tunnels come together. Then they go off every which way.

The tunnel entrances all look pretty much the same. We had marked the ones we'd explored on our map. Tonight there was only the farthest part of Tunnel Thirteen left to do. I knew right where to find it. I ran over and called the others. "Over here, you guys. This is it." In the shadowy light, I saw Xela take a deep breath.

"Don't worry, Xela," Rubi said in a soothing voice. "I'm right behind you."

"I know, Rubi," she replied. "I've got my eye on you."

\*     \*     \*

I loved these tunnels. I lived to explore them. The dark, shadowy passageways. The tiny walled-off rooms. The stairs that lead nowhere. The strange markings on the walls. It was like we were in some bizarre, lost world. Suddenly, Xela stopped. "Listen," she whispered.

We crouched behind some rubble. I covered the light stick with two of my hands. "I don't hear anything," Rubi murmured.

"Then listen harder," said Xela. I could hear the hum of the underground reactors. The drip of sludge as it hit the floor. Nothing strange about that. Then suddenly, a grinding, raspy noise. Rubi stood up to take a look.

"Duck!" Xela screamed. Rubi stooped down just as hundreds of flying Scrapebotz came hurtling through the tunnel. Their cries were deafening. They passed so close, their wings brushed against my face. Then silence. Shaking—but only just a little—I got up. "I hate those things."

"It's hard to love something that eats crud off of walls for a living," Rubi said.

"Last chance to turn back," offered Xela.

"Too late," I had to admit. "I think I took a wrong turn."

"What? Again?" asked Rubi.

"Hey, if you don't like the way I lead, you do it. Think of all the times my little wrong turns have gotten us some place great."

"Yeah? Like the slime pits? Or the acid-spewing bog?"

"Like I said, all the good places."

Rubi shrugged. "You've got a point, Arms. Lead on."

"Besides," I said, "it's not my fault. I'm used to the way things are on the surface. Orderly. But down here, there's no pattern. Everything's all mixed up." It was true. Just like on my own planet of Armegettem, everything on the surface of Roma was pretty predictable. No matter which way you turned, you always knew where you were. But The Tunnels were a different story. They were a labyrinth. A maze. One wrong turn and you might never see daylight again. That's what made them soooo cool!

Rubi turned to Xela and me and winked. "I happen to know The Tunnels were here long before the school."

"Really, professor," I said. "And how do you know that?"

"I have my sources. Been checking around. Seems this place used to be a prison."

"A *prison?*" Xela exclaimed. "When did you find this out?"

"I've known for a while, but I didn't want to scare you."

Xela laughed nervously. "Oh, so you save it for

now, when we're in the deepest, spookiest part of this place? Thanks a lot."

"Don't worry," I said. "That was all millions of years ago. Right, Rubi?"

"Well, a while ago anyway. Before the Planetary Union. Back when Roma was just a barren asteroid. Planets dumped their worst criminals into these tunnels."

I figured Rubi was just trying to scare us. I winked back at him. "So I guess they're all just roaming around, huh?"

"Nah," he replied. "Thousands of years went by before they decided to make Roma the garden spot of the Universe. There's no way any of them are left."

"But," I squeaked, "some life forms live thousands of years."

Suddenly there was a blood-curdling scream! Xela was gone! Rubi and I raced through the dim light of the tunnel, yelling "Xela!" No answer. We shouted again.

She was nowhere to be found. I felt horrible. She said she didn't want to come tonight. She knew something would go wrong.

Another scream! Very close this time. But from where? The sound echoed off the walls. It was all around us!

"Which way do we go?" I cried. "Xela, where are you?"

Xela stepped from the shadows, laughing so hard she could barely stand. "Looking for me?"

"Xela Zim Bareen, that was not funny," I declared.

"I told you something weird would happen tonight," Xela said, grinning.

"Too weird for me," I said. "I'm heading back."

That's when we heard it. Big, floppy footsteps slapping across the wet floor. And they were getting closer. A heavy door slammed. Voices! Coming this way.

"Probably maintenance breffels on their patrols," Rubi whispered. "They'll report us! We've got to hide!"

Xela got up and darted off. "This way!"

"Xela, wait!" I cried. But it was too late. She'd vanished in the shadows. We had no choice but to follow. We couldn't leave her alone. The footsteps were coming faster now.

"I think they heard us!" Rubi rasped.

We found Xela in a dark and narrow alley. "Xela, come back," Rubi begged. "We'll be caught!"

The footsteps were almost on top of us now. The breffels' headlamps were already lighting up the entrance to the alley. Desperate, we followed Xela, hoping the shadows would hide us. Xela moved forward, stopping at . . . a dead end!

I panicked . . . until I looked into Xela's eyes. She was completely calm. Smiling, she said, "Let me show you something." Then she gave the solid rock wall behind us a shove. It opened!

Xela pushed us inside just as the breffels entered the alley. The heavy stone door shut with a whoosh. We could hear the breffels' voices as they turned away. Totally baffled.

I picked myself up off the floor and gave Xela a full-press hug. "Saved! How did you know this was here?"

"I found it by accident. When I went to hide from you."

I held up the light stick.

"What is this place, anyway?" Rubi asked.

It seemed to be some sort of abandoned laboratory. Filled with ancient equipment covered with dust. Except that at one end of the room there was a wall-sized computer screen. And it was on.

# 4

## Xela Zim Bareen

A pale purple light was coming from the blank screen, throwing weird, unnatural shadows onto the cave-like walls. Outdated equipment, some of it heaped into tangled piles, littered the floor. Along one wall was a makeshift workbench. It was covered with colorful strands of wire that were hopelessly twisted around pieces of useless-looking machinery. "Roma-rama!" exclaimed Arms as she looked around.

"Way to go," said Rubi, flashing me a grin.

And I had to admit, it was. I mean, who would have thought I'd find this place? Me? Xela. The good girl. The brain child. The one everyone relies on to be responsible. All by myself I'd discovered the coolest, creepiest part of The Tunnels. This was definitely the best!

I started wandering around, picking up strange artifacts from a long wall of floor-to-ceiling shelves carved into the rock walls. I laughed. "This place looks like the Museum of Worthless Matter." It did. The shelves were filled with, well, who knows . . . none of us had ever seen stuff like this before.

"Any idea what this could be?" I asked as I picked up a grayish white tube. One end was rounded and stitched closed, while the other end had an opening you could slip a hand or a foot into. That was it, except for a ragged hole at the halfway point. "Looks like a leftover from the last intergalactic garage sale," Rubi said.

"Well, whatever it is, there's lots of them." And there were. A big pile of them, some small, some large, some in patterns and bright colors, but mostly in white, black, brown and blue. None of them matched.

"Looks to me like they are some kind of sleeping pouches for shimmers," Rubi said.

"No," I shrugged. "Too ugly for that."

"Well, I know what this is," Rubi said as he reached for the shelf closest to him. He picked up a soft, floppy piece of shaped brown cloth and plopped it on top of his tentacles. "Head gear! What do you think, Arms?"

"Very handsome, Rubi," Arms mumbled without looking up. She was bent over the computer controls.

"Hey, put it back, Rubi," I warned. "What if whoever works here comes back?" I didn't want to ruin the fun, but there was a half-eaten bowl of thick green glooble on a table near me. And it was still warm to the touch.

"Maybe we should go," I suggested as gently as I could. "Ready, Arms?"

But Arms just ignored me. "Too cool" was all she said.

"What's too cool?" Rubi asked.

"This computer. It's a Moc-tash one-zero-zero-nine. I've never seen one of these—only read about them. They haven't been used for light years. The weird thing is, someone's grafted a neuro-net skin onto the old-style plasma drives. Must be what's keeping this thing alive!"

"Maybe this *is* some kind of museum," I said.

Arms shook her head. "If this were a museum, don't you think we'd know about it? No, this is some kind of secret lab."

"That does it," I said. "We're leaving. Come on, Arms. Get up."

"Okay, but I'd sure like a chance to use this thing," Arms said as she stood.

That's when it happened. One of Arms's arms accidentally hit the computer's control panel. The thing began to sputter and whir. Shadowy figures filled the screen. The background went from pale purple to a dense shade of blue. And weird, unworldly looking images began to scroll across the screen. "Aaaahhh!" was all Rubi and I could say.

"Incredible," whispered Arms. And I had to admit it was. There on the screen were pictures and words that seemed to be about secret missions to planets outside the Union. At first the information came scrolling slowly across the screen. Then suddenly, it started moving faster and faster!

"Shut it off, Arms!" I shouted. "We'll be boiled alive if anyone knows we've seen this stuff!"

"I'm trying!" said Arms.

"Try harder," I cried.

"Here it is! I think I've got it. The shut-off switch. We should be out of here in no time." The images on the screen began to slow down. And as they did, I heard Arms gasp. There, on the screen, was a picture of an alien from Planet RU1:2. It had smooth skin, straight hair, two eyes, one nose, and no scales.

"Gogol," Arms whispered.

"Or someone who looks just like him," said Rubi.

"I don't understand," I murmured. "Gogol told me he was one of a kind, that no other creature in the universe looks like him. Not even on his home planet."

"Well," Rubi said, "he's either a liar, or something really weird is going on."

"Like what?" Arms asked.

"I don't know," said Rubi. "We'll have to ask Gogol."

# 5

## Rubidoux

I was exhausted by the time I got back to the dorm.
But there was no way I could sleep. It would have
been incredible enough to find the abandoned lab;
it was by far the coolest discovery we'd made in
The Tunnels. But it was the thought of Gogol that
kept me tossing and turning all night. What was his
secret? Why had he lied to us? What if he was a
spy from a violent world sent to learn the secrets
of the Planetary Union? Or maybe his real looks
were so horrible he'd taken on his current shape to
hide how disgusting he was. Whatever the story,
there was no way I was going to let him get away
with hiding the truth.

By the time the hitsu chimed, I was up, dressed, and headed toward the cafeteria in search of Gogol. I'd never really paid much attention to the guy before. It was a mystery to me which food line he'd be in. Because of his nose, I thought he might be a carbon-based creature like me. But today I wasn't letting his looks fool me. They could be a disguise.

I started by checking out the line for silicon-based life forms. No easy feat, believe me. The stench coming off their slimy soups and tar-like blue-plate specials made my tentacles stand up and quiver. Gogol wasn't there.

Next, I tried the section reserved for polymer-based eaters. You know, the ones who mix radioactive powdered minerals, then suck them up with a straw. It's enough to make you grateful for the macaroni and cheese they serve to carbon-based life forms at every meal. But again no luck. No Gogol.

I decided to skip the line with the Bottom Feeders. I just couldn't bring myself to look. I won't go into any heavy descriptions. All I need to say is that She-Rak's a BF.

Suddenly I heard, "Rubidoux! Over here!" I looked to my left and saw Arms waving all four of her arms. She's hard to miss in a crowd.

"So, have you seen him yet?" I asked as I took my seat at the table.

"Xela went to get him," Arms said, lowering her

voice. I could see she was as nervous as I was. "What do you think he's going to say?"

"I don't know, but I . . ."

"Hi Arms, Rubi. Gogol agreed to join us for a while," Xela said.

Gogol took a seat. He had a wary look on his face. Maybe he wasn't sure if he should eat the chopped beet soup on his tray. His eyes moved from Xela past Arms, then fixed on me. I could tell from his look, I was not his favorite alien life form. "What's this all about? Xela said you had something important to tell me."

I took a deep breath. It was now or never. "I do, but first we want to ask you some questions. Xela says you told her that no one else in the universe looks like you. Is that true?"

Gogol looked hard at Xela. He didn't say a word. I tried to read his thoughts. But they were locked up tight.

"You have to trust me, Gogol. Tell them," Xela said.

Gogol looked down for several seconds. He was tense. There was no doubt about it. I could actually feel him trying to decide what to do. Then, slowly, he began to speak. "What Xela told you is true. There is no one on my home planet that looks like me. They're all reptilian. I'm not. I came to DUH so I could find others like me, to solve the mystery

25

of my origin. But, as you know, there are no creatures here that look like me, either."

"Ever search through the planetary database?" Arms asked.

"Of course. Nothing. I just have to accept that I am a mutant," Gogol replied.

"I don't believe it," I blurted out. "I think you're hiding something. Like maybe you don't want to admit where you're really from." I just had to get him to come clean.

"Rubi!" Xela gasped. "I can't believe you said that."

"Come on, Xela. Knowing what we know, how can you buy this bunk?"

Gogol seethed. "I don't know what you *think* you know, but I can tell you what you don't know. You have no idea what it's like growing up in a world where no one else looks like you. Where you never feel like you fit in. A place where others act like they accept you, but they really think you are a freak. And so you spend your whole life searching for answers, trying to find some place in the universe, *any* place, where you can feel at home. You don't know how hard I worked to get here. Diplomatic Universal Headquarters is the only place where being different doesn't make me stand out. And it's the best place for me to try to understand where I come from. Now that I'm here, I don't need some self-important Douxwhopian making trouble for me."

The three of us just looked at him. We were stunned. He had a right to be angry. I was embarrassed. I shouldn't have confronted him like that.

"I'm sorry, Gogol. We're not trying to make trouble for you," I said. "In fact, I think we can help you."

"What do you mean?" he asked.

"Gogol," Arms said carefully. "We saw a life form that looks like you."

"What?" Gogol said with a start. "That's impossible. Where?"

"We can't say any more here," I said keeping my voice down. "Meet us at midnight at Gate Fifty-One, behind the power center, and you'll find out."

"Gate Fifty-One? There is no Gate Fifty-One," Gogol said. He looked over at Xela.

"It's okay, Gogol," she said. "I'll go with you."

# 6

## Rubidoux

Gate Fifty-One is not listed on any map. So it wasn't surprising that Gogol had never heard of it. Not many had. You have to know to go behind the power center. From there you follow the ditch that runs along the outer wall of the school to find our secret way into The Tunnels. And, of course, the stench keeps most people away.

I got to the entrance to The Tunnels right at midnight. Xela and Gogol looked like they'd been there awhile. "You two must have gotten here early."

Xela was jumping up and down, hugging herself against the cold. "A full ikron now. Gogol insisted."

I looked at Gogol. In spite of his big speech, I

still didn't trust the guy. In the glow from the ditch I could see that his cheeks were flushed and his eyes were wide with anticipation. Even those furry things above his eyelids were arched up high. If he was scared about going into The Tunnels, he wasn't showing it. He was definitely stoked.

"So you came," I said.

"When do we leave?" was all Gogol said.

"Just as soon as Arms—"

"Sorry," called out Arms, as she ran up to us. "Didn't mean to be the last one. I wanted to get an extra light stick for Gogol."

"Thanks," said Gogol, not sounding too grateful. "Now let's get going."

"It's not quite that easy," I said.

"Yeah," said Arms. "We need to break in . . . oops, I mean, undo the bolts. But never fear, four-armed Arms is here. Someone hand me the wrench."

"That's not quite what I meant," I said. "I don't think we should go anywhere until we swear Gogol to secrecy."

Gogol took a menacing step toward me. "You don't trust me?"

"I just want to be sure you understand that this is no game. We're risking expulsion here. You have to swear by the six stars of Erin that you will keep this an absolute secret. You can tell no one where you've been and what you've seen. Do you swear?"

29

I sounded so serious, I scared myself. But we'd nearly been caught the night before. Why, I kept asking myself, was I risking all for this guy?

Gogol hesitated. "I swear."

"By Erin," I said.

"By the six stars," agreed Gogol.

"And another thing . . ."

"Come on," said Arms. "The Tunnels will erode away at this rate." Then she switched on her light stick and took off. Xela followed.

I turned to Gogol. "Go where I go. Move when I move. Don't try any funny stuff. One wrong turn in these tunnels and you're lost forever. Got it?"

"Got it, boss," said Gogol with a sneer. Geez, this guy was getting on my cranial nerves. *I'd love to know what Xela sees in him,* I thought. Even now, walking through The Tunnels, he was quiet, withdrawn. Off in his own little world, wherever in the universe that might be.

Xela tried to reassure him. "Relax, Gogol. There's not really much to worry about down here."

"That's true," Arms piped up. "If you don't mind slime bogs, flying Scrapebotz, and breffel patrols."

"Thanks so much, Arms," said Xela.

"It's okay, Xela," said Gogol. "I'm not afraid AAAAGH!" Gogol's scream was the last thing we heard as he disappeared from sight.

"Gogol?" yelled Xela. "Answer me. Where are you?" Nothing. Not a sound. Just the plip-plop of sludge hitting the floor.

"Xela," I said. "If this is one of your jokes . . ."

"Are you kidding?" cried Xela. "He's gone, Rubi. For real. Come on! We've got to find him!" Xela started to run back down the tunnel.

"Xela, freeze!" Arms said in a commanding whisper, her eyes glued to the floor. "Both of you! Don't move!"

"Why?" I asked.

"Don't you see it? There. Where you're about to step. Where Gogol stepped a second ago."

I strained to see the ground below me, but even with my light stick, I didn't see anything unusual. I started to move toward Arms.

"I'm telling you not to move!" Arms shifted her light stick to her lower hand. It lit up the ground like daylight. And then I saw it. Tiny cracks. Hairline thin. Covering the floor like a green-horned araknoid's web.

"Watch!" said Arms, as she crouched down and pushed her light stick into the ground. Sure enough, it began to suck it up. "Something must have happened since we were here last. Maybe an underground tremor."

"Whatever it was, Gogol's down there. And we've got to do something," I said.

"Go for help?" asked Xela, who had carefully made her way back to where Arms and I were standing.

"Go after him," I said, more bravely than I felt.

"What?" asked Arms in disbelief.

"Look," I said as I reached my arm through the floor. "I noticed when you stuck your light stick in, it's hollow on the other side. I think it's a crust bubble and will lead us to another tunnel. We've got to go through it."

"Rubi, I think the lack of air down here has gone to your brain."

"Look, how else are we going to find Gogol? At least if we follow him, wherever he went, we'll all be together. We've got maps. We'll be able to find our way out."

"This is a very bad idea," said Xela.

"Come on," I said, jumping in. "Last one in is a rotten efru."

Sometimes I wonder about my bright ideas. Now was one of those times. I was being hurled through a long, black tunnel, pulled by a powerful undertow, at what felt like P-force speed. My stomach was in my throat. My cheeks ached from having my skin stretched back behind my hearing ports. And all around me, all I could hear were the screams of Xela and Arms. Just when I felt like my cells were exploding, I hit bottom. Hard. I was lying on the ground with the wind knocked out of me.

"Aaahhhhh." Arms fell on top of me. "Rubi? Is that you?" she asked.

"I think so," I answered. "Where's Xela?"

"Over here," squeaked a little voice from the other side of the . . . who knew where we were?

"Anyone's light stick work?" asked Xela.

"Mine, I think," said Gogol.

"Gogol!" screamed Arms.

"Keep it down," I cautioned. "There could be breffels!"

"Gogol!" Arms whispered. "We're so happy to see you, kind of, sort of."

At that moment Gogol got his light stick on. "Look!" whispered Xela. "We're in the Crisscross. There's Tunnel Thirteen!"

"You must have the luck of the Kronish with you, Gogol," I said as I got up and brushed myself off.

"Well, come on then," said Xela. "It's on to lucky number thirteen."

Sticking together like glooble, we followed the twists and turns of Tunnel Thirteen. Arms attempted to lighten things up by chattering on about her science class. She was deep into a story about someone named Blimpron. "You know," she was saying, "the girl who leaves the slime trail. She told the professor to mix them both together and *then* heat it up . . ."

33

I was only half listening. My eyes were on Gogol. I just had to figure out how this guy was wired. Why no fear when The Tunnels were so scary? Had he been here before? Was this a trap? I was willing to bet he'd like nothing better than to turn us in to the authorities. That would really make him a hero. Claimed he was the only one like him in the universe. Yeah, right.

"Gogol," I asked in my most innocent voice, "is your neural map on file in the library?"

"Yes," he said, "but I choose to have the file locked down."

"Figures."

"Are you concerned about how I think?"

"Let's just say curious."

"I'm seventy percent water if that helps," he said.

Actually, that explained a lot.

We walked the rest of the way without saying much. Xela's third eye watched for breffels. Finally, we got to the corridor that leads to the lab. We walked down the narrow passageway and stopped. Gogol stared at the blank rock wall in front of him. Then he turned on me. "Is this your idea of a joke?"

If he was faking anger, he was pretty good. I swear I saw steam coming out of his ears. Xela touched his arm and smiled. "I wouldn't do that to you, Gogol." Then she leaned on the wall, just as she had the night before. Once again, the secret entrance was revealed.

"After you," I said to Gogol.

"Sorry." Gogol shrugged. "Guess I'm kind of tense." Could have fooled me.

# 7

## Gogol

I'd thought from the beginning that I never should have come. Their "big secret" confirmed it. A huge cave-like room filled with dust and a bunch of junk. For this I risked expulsion? Rubi was behind this. I could feel it. He'd love nothing better than to make a fool of me. But Xela? She'd always been so . . . so . . . different. The one true friend I'd had at Roma. Why had I trusted her? I'd promised myself I'd never tell anyone my secret. Well, I had. And now I was paying the price. Still, if they did know something. . . . I made my face a blank. I didn't want Rubi locking in on my thoughts. "So this is what you wanted to show me?"

"No," said Arms, as she pushed by me. "It's on the computer." The screen was blank, but Arms's hands were flying. "I printed out a manual for this thing. We should be up in no time."

"Good," said Xela. "This place gives me the creeps. I keep expecting something or someone to come slamming through that door."

She wasn't the only one expecting visitors. Why had they brought me here? Arms, for one, wasn't giving anything away. All she said was, "Xela, calm down. It's the middle of the night. No one would be working now."

"I might believe you," Xela mumbled, "except the bowl of green glooble is gone."

"Did you see this?" Rubi asked, obviously trying to divert my attention. He was holding up a long black box. "It's an ancient WAT-Man, a Warp-Time Manipulator. This is how they would lock in wormholes for intergalactic travel before they invented the way we use now. I wonder if it works."

Rubi turned the unit on. It whirred and sparked and glowed. "Hey, don't play with that!" cried Xela. "Next thing you know we'll all get sucked up and dumped into some deserted mining colony in Quadrant Z."

"Don't worry, Xela. Nothing happens unless you enter a destination," Rubi said. But he put it down anyway. "How's it going, Arms?" he asked.

"Well, I thought I had it, but this thing has been

messed with so much I'm going to need a little more time."

I walked over to the shelves filled with what seemed to be ancient artifacts. Rubi must have had the same idea, because he reached over and put a brown, floppy hat on his head. "Ah, my favorite head gear," he said. Then turning to me he asked, "Seen one of these before?"

Now how was I supposed to have . . . that's when the chill passed down my spine. For some reason, I had no idea why, I knew precisely what Rubi was wearing. "It's called a fedora."

"A fedora?" said Rubi. "Who ever heard of that? I guess I have to give you credit for imagination," he added. Then he came over and stared right at me. "Gogol, are you okay? You're pale as a ghost."

"I don't know. It's this stuff. It's all so strange, but somehow familiar. Like I already know what it is. But how could I?"

"Yeah? Well, do you recognize this?" Rubi picked up a metallic ring with a chunk of stamped metal and a piece of leather hanging off it. The chill went down my spine again. I could feel the blood drain from my face. "Those are keys," I said slowly. "Lost keys from a '57 Chevy."

"What's a Chevy?" asked Rubi. I never did get a chance to tell him. Just at that moment, Arms yelled, "I got it! Told you I'd do it."

Xela smiled. "Arms, we never doubted you."

Suddenly the screen came alive with information—maps, charts, pictures. "I think you were right, Rubi. This is some kind of database of worlds outside of the Union," Arms said.

"Yeah," Rubi said excitedly. "Looks like all the cool war-torn places."

Xela gave a weak little laugh. "That's kind of scary."

"What's this got to do with me?" I asked.

"Hold on, Gogol. I just need to enter RU1:2 and hit search," Arms said. The screen went blank for a second. Then . . .

I gasped. The shock of recognition shook my whole body. For the first time ever, I was staring at a picture of a creature that was clearly my own species. Tears welled up in my eyes. My mouth was open, but no words came out. I couldn't move. When I finally felt calm enough to speak, I choked out "Where is this?" in a whisper.

"This is a sample of a life form from Planet RU1:2," said Arms.

I moved closer to the computer. "Is there any more data about RU1:2?"

"I'm sure there is," Arms said. "I think we just scroll through by pressing the down key . . ."

Without warning, an earsplitting alarm went off!

# 8

## Arms Akimbo

"Arms, what's happening?" Gogol yelled. He was standing one inch from my ear and screaming at the top of his lungs. Okay, sure, the alarm was loud, but back off a little! I shot him a look.

"I don't know," I shouted back at him—politely. "The computer must have been rigged!"

"Well, stop it!" pleaded Gogol as he came even closer. He sure didn't look too good. There was a wild look in his eyes. A panic. He'd come so close to learning about his past, I guess he couldn't stand the thought of letting this chance get away. I didn't want to let him down!

My four arms and twenty-four fingers were working overtime. I know that to other life forms it looks like I'm flailing all over the place. But this is when I'm at my best. Every action, every movement, completely planned and controlled. Well, okay, maybe not *every* move. I can be a little klutzy at times. But right now I was being amazing. I pressed every button, pulled every lever, and flicked every switch. But the alarm continued to blare.

"Forget it, Arms!" yelled Rubi, tugging on my shirt. "We've got to get out of here. NOW!"

I hate to lose! I knew I could figure this out. But I also knew Rubi was right. Time was up. Xela and Rubi turned and ran. I was close behind. But no Gogol. When we reached the door, we all looked back. Gogol had picked up something from the workbench and was furiously jabbing at it. He moved to the center of the lab. As he did, he kept looking at the data on the frozen computer screen. He was no longer panicked. In fact, he looked strangely relaxed.

"Gogol! Let's go!" Xela begged.

"Is he doing what I think he's doing?" I asked Rubi. I didn't want to hear the answer.

"Afraid so," said Rubi. "Looks like he's entering the coordinates from the screen into the WAT-Man."

"Why would he do that?" Xela asked in disbelief. Before Rubi or I had a chance to answer, a new sound split the air.

41

"Coordinates for Planet RU1:2 confirmed. Stand by for warp-time travel."

It was the computer. Gogol had locked in a wormhole that would take him to Planet RU1:2.

"We've got to stop him," Xela shouted. "If he goes and we get caught, the only jobs we'll get will be waxing space roamers for the rest of our lives."

Rubi nodded and lunged across the room, screaming, "Gogol! Stop!"

The next few seconds seemed to take place in slow motion. The computer announced pleasantly, "Wormhole materializing." And sure enough, right in front of Gogol an intergalactic gateway opened. Invisible waves, like the rings that roll out when a pebble hits water, began to ripple through the air. A jolt of ice-cold wind filled the room. Gogol took a step toward the entrance. Rubi grabbed his collar. "WARNING!" blared the computer, not so pleasantly now. "Wormhole unstable! Do not enter!"

"You can't go, Gogol. It's not safe!" Xela cried.

Gogol looked over his shoulder at us. "I have to!"

Rubi tried his hardest to pull Gogol back. But Gogol threw himself into the wormhole. He must have caught Rubi off balance, because the next thing we knew, he'd tumbled into the void, too.

Xela and I watched in horror as the wormhole disappeared and the room fell silent. "No!" yelled Xela, charging to the spot where our friends had been standing. "RUBI! GOGOL!" she screamed into the empty air.

"Xela, it will be okay," I said as calmly as I could. "We'll get them back." I watched as the light in Xela's prism-like eye went dim.

"We have to!" she said.

# 9

## Rubidoux

I was still gripping Gogol's collar when we began to rematerialize, but the shock of hitting a cold, hard surface made me let go. "Ow!" said Gogol, as I tumbled over him. "Watch out!"

"Watch out?" I said. "Watch out? You watch out. You're the one who dragged me here!"

"I didn't ask you to come."

"Never mind that. You need to get us back. NOW!"

Gogol was looking around. If he'd heard me, he didn't show it. "Where do you think we are?" he whispered.

"I have no idea. I'm just glad there are no other life forms here."

We were crouched together in the middle of a long, narrow passageway. Bright yellow light from a Class Seven star filtered through clear squares that ran along the top of the walls. A few of these squares were angled to create openings in the walls and crisp, moist atmospheric gases were wafting through them. Cautiously, I took a sniff.

Ah! Nitrogen, oxygen, hydrogen, and thank goodness, a touch of ozone. Ozone is the one common element in atmospheres throughout the universe. It's what makes all of us able to breathe each other's air.

"Gogol, do you have any idea how much trouble we're in? Call that wormhole back right now!" I tried to get the WAT-Man out of his hand, but he scooted across the hard black-and-tan squares and sat with his back to me.

"Rubidoux," he pleaded, "just give me a little time."

"The coordinates for Roma are 7QZ dot 3," I said, sliding over by him.

"Please?" he said.

One look at him and I remembered why we were here. Gogol was on a quest. He *had* to know who he was. So we had probably landed on a hostile world. So it was a little dangerous. So's falling through a crust bubble. I could give him a little time.

"Fine," I told him. "Half an ikron. Then we're gone."

"No problem," he agreed. "But we're a little too out in the open here. We need to find a hiding place."

"No kidding," I said as I leaned my back against the wall. It shifted with a loud CLANG!

"Shhh!" commanded Gogol. "You might wake them."

"Who? What are you talking about?"

"Whoever, or whatever, lives behind that door you just leaned against," he said pointing behind me.

I turned and saw that I had been cozying up to a small metal door. It was narrow and short with slots for air cut into it near the top. There was an identical door stacked above it. In fact, now that I looked, I could see that the entire passageway was lined with them. There were hundreds!

"Gogol, are you telling me this is where your relatives sleep?"

"I don't know," he said, examining one. "Maybe these are like cocoons. Maybe we landed in a hatchery or something."

I tried to look through the slots at the top of the door nearest to me. "Whew! Get a load of this one! It smells terrible. I think something died in here!"

"Rubi, look at this," said Gogol, pulling on a handle. "They're locked. It's a jail."

"And they just leave the bodies in there until they rot? How barbaric!"

"Hey," said Gogol, "this one's unlocked." I

looked over in time to see Gogol begin to lift the latch on one of the upper compartments.

"Gogol, stop!" I blurted in a desperate whisper. But it was too late. A horrible alarm began to sound. Suddenly, wooden rectangles up and down the passageway came flying open! Loud, two-legged creatures started moving toward us from both directions. There was nowhere to run. Nowhere to hide. I froze.

But not Gogol. He just stood there relaxed as could be, beaming from one weird-shaped ear to the other. And why not? All these creatures resembled him. Thankfully, he began fiddling with the WAT-Man.

"Good idea, Gogol. Get us out of here! Now!"

"Are you kidding? I'm not leaving. I just want to get the pan-tawky translators working so we can communicate with them. Here, put one on."

The pan-tawky must have started working, because I understood the next thing that was said to me. "Hey, stretch. That's my locker you're guarding."

I looked down on a short Gogol-like creature with red hair and an attitude. "Don't open that," I warned. "Something died in there."

Red just brushed past me. With a couple of flicks of his wrist he unlocked the lower door and swung it open, nearly hitting me. A few of his friends were standing around watching us. They looked at me with less than friendly stares. And no wonder. I didn't blend in as well as Gogol. For one thing, I was head and shoulders taller than everyone else. And though the color of my bronze skin seemed to be within their normal range, mine shimmered. Add to that purple tentacles hanging below the brim of my so-called fedora, and you can understand why I was attracting some attention.

Red-with-an-attitude pulled something out of the locker. Holding up the same kind of white tube with a hole we'd seen in the lab on Roma he said, "That smell is my gym socks." Then he reached inside the door again and pulled out something else. "And my lunch. Got a problem with that?"

He slammed the door and walked away. One of his friends sneered back at me. "What a dork!"

I don't think he meant it as a compliment. Though it could have been. I've always been fond of the sweet, furry dor-kus that populate the planet of Blather. "Well, what do you know?" I said to Gogol. "They have dor-kus here." But there was no answer. "Gogol?" I said, beginning to look around in a panic. *Fine for him to mingle with the locals,* I thought, *but I don't exactly fit in.* That little fact didn't seem to bother Gogol. He was nowhere to be found.

There was nothing for me to do but begin to cruise the passageway. I tried crouching down so I'd fit in with the other two-legged creatures, but if I did that, there was no chance I'd see Gogol. All I could think to do was duck into a doorway and try and keep my cool. That's when I spied him. He was across the way, talking with one of the RU1:2ians. From where I stood she looked to be female, with curly yellow hair coming off her scalp, long sparkly prisms embedded in her earlobes, and a floppy, floor-length costume. The prisms looked similar to Xela's third eye. I guessed that meant they were a sign of superior hearing.

In spite of all the creatures moving between us, I could hear the female's voice above the noise. "Are you new here?" she was asking.

"Oh, yes," said Gogol. "And I love it."

"Really?" she asked. "I moved here like in the middle of the year, from California you know, and I don't really get the local frame of mind. I figure all this rain gives them water on the brain, if you know what I mean."

"Oh, yes," Gogol said, beaming. "Seventy percent."

"If you say so."

The passageway was finally clearing. I made my way over to Gogol. He said hello as if nothing had happened. All the female said was, "Wow!"

"Wow?" I asked.

"Uh-huh! I mean I've heard of body piercing and tatoos, but I've never seen skin dyeing and purple dreadlocks! You are soooo cool!" I felt my whole body begin to relax.

"So are you two on your way to the caf?" the female of the species asked.

Gogol looked at me. I knew what he was thinking. Our pan-tawky translator told us a calf was a young cow. RU1:2ians were obviously ruled by a cow!

Gogol shrugged. "Take us to your leader."

"Boy, you two are funny. Where did you say you're from?"

"Roma," said Gogol.

"Oh, Italians. That explains it. My parents said they're going to take me there for high school graduation. Maybe I could come visit you!" Gogol and I exchanged worried looks. The female didn't seem to notice. She just kept right on talking, saying things like, "Oh. I'm sorry. Didn't mean to invite myself. I don't even know your names. How could I stay with you? I'm Rebecca. Who are you?"

"I'm Gogol and this is Rubi."

"That's short for Rubidoux," I chimed in.

"Wow. Your name is soooo cool."

I looked into Rebecca's deep, blue eyes and thought, maybe RU1:2ians weren't so bad after all. But then, I hadn't seen The Calf.

"I'm having Sloppy Joes. What about you?" Rebecca asked as I stood behind her in line.

I was staring down at a lumpy brown mush that

smelled worse than things that She-Rak eats. That's when I knew in my hearts that this planet wasn't for me. "Do they have macaroni and cheese?" I asked hopefully.

"Only on Fridays," said Rebecca. "Here. Try some pizza." She flopped a limp wedge of red and pale yellow food stuff on my tray.

"Gogol," I hissed. "I can't eat this stuff."

"Are you kidding?" he said. "It all looks great to me."

Rebecca could see I was looking pretty pale for someone who's bronze. "Oops," she said, apologizing. "Imagine me giving pizza to a real Italian. I'm sorry." Then she took it off my plate. "I've heard people say America has the worst food on Earth. You know, our British ancestry and stuff. And Italy. It's supposed to have some of the best. No wonder you can't eat."

*Earth?* I thought. *We're on Earth?* "Gogol," I whispered. "We've landed on a dying planet. We *have* to get out of here now!"

"I can't," he said. "I have to learn as much as I can about this place." Then turning to Rebecca, he asked in his sweetest voice, "Will you take me to the golden arches, please?"

"Love to," she said. She was obviously religious. "Maybe, like um, we could go after school."

*Oh great*, I thought. *Once he ate soul food, he'd never want to leave.*

# 10

## Arms Akimbo

Once Xela and I faced what we were up against, we got busy. Me at the computer. Xela looking for something that could help us bring Rubi and Gogol home.

"Arms, I can't find anything useful on this workbench," Xela told me sadly. "You'd think there'd be another WAT-Man somewhere in this mess. How's it going with you?"

"Okay. No problem. I can do this. Have them back in no time," I said with a laugh.

Xela came over to where I was sitting at the computer. Then she locked those two huge eyes on me. "Arms, the truth."

"This is going to be harder than I thought," I sighed. "The manual I printed out only helps me with the basics. This computer's been changed so many times I'm not sure what's what."

"Oh, great. Look Arms, we need to go for help."

"Xela, I promise you we will not leave our friends stranded on some distant . . ."

"Possibly violent."

"Okay, Xela, possibly violent, planet. But please, I'm begging you, let me see if I can bring them back first. If I can, we'll get out of this mess without ruining our lives. If I can't, I'll be the first one to go ask for help."

"I don't know, Arms. I feel so guilty. Like this is all my fault. We should never have brought Gogol here. He . . ."

"Xela, get real. Nobody told him to mail himself across the galaxy. Besides, I'm more worried about Rubi than Gogol. From what we've seen of the data, Rubi doesn't look too much like the creatures on RU1:2. How's he going to fit in? Here," I said handing her the manual, "see if it gives the equations for deep space warp."

"Okay," Xela said as she picked it up and started flipping through it. "But I don't understand why they can't just get back using the WAT-Man they took with them."

"I'm not totally sure they can't. But I know that some of the older units only worked for one-way travel. They relied on home base to bring them back. There's a chance that old hand-held unit was updated, but I don't think we want to wait to find out."

Xela tossed down the manual. "Arms, maybe this stuff makes sense to you, but to me it's total gibberish. I think the key to bringing them back is hidden somewhere in this room. And we've got to find it!"

Xela got up and began to circle the room. I was so busy I didn't bother to look up, even when Xela yelled, "I found it!" She slid open the door to a compartment on the main computer drive. Air colder than the dark side of Zedoria spilled into the room.

"Arms, what are these?" she asked as I gasped from the cold. I looked over just in time to see Xela reach toward the cobalt blue canisters stacked three deep inside the compartment.

"Don't touch them!" I cried.

Startled, Xela quickly drew back her hand. "Why not?"

"They're Think-U-Bators. Outdated now by a hundred years, they once connected computers in a network of virtual intelligence."

"So why can't I touch them?"

"They are kept at minus 420 degrees. Touch them and your fingers will stick. Freeze dry. Then fall off. All in about three seconds."

"Okay, I don't really need to know any more

about those. But how come *you* know about all this ancient stuff?"

"Guess 'cause I read a lot," I said, shrugging. "Look, I got the Think-U-Bators on line! This changes everything. Xela, I think we can do this."

"How?"

"It's pretty easy actually. When Gogol and Rubi were reassembled on the other end of who-knows-where, their molecules were imprinted with the wormhole's unique signature. Every wormhole has one. The main computer uses the energy pathway created by the wormhole to detect any creatures imprinted with its code. Then, presto, gizorto, we push a button and, poof! They are standing here in seconds. Like they never left."

"Do you think this computer can handle it?"

"I think so. I just need to figure out how to find the target coordinates. Then we hit the reclaim button."

"But Arms, just before they disappeared, the computer said the wormhole was unstable."

"All right," I confessed. "So we have one teensy-weensy worry. But you have to figure we're not dealing with the usual well-traveled highways and trade routes here. What we've got resembles a primitive road on a jungle planet. It twists and turns. It's narrow and bumpy. And sometimes the bridge is out. So?"

"What do you mean, 'Sometimes the bridge is out,'?" asked Xela quietly.

"What I mean is that when you are in an unstable wormhole, there's always the chance it can collapse."

"Oh, great."

# 11

## Rubidoux

By the time we left the food line, Gogol's tray was piled high with Earthling intake substances. I did a quick scan. Just as I suspected, its nutrient value was zero. I took a pass.

Rebecca insisted we join her at her table. She wanted us to meet some of her "buds." They may be named for young flowers, but these Earthlings aren't really much to look at. For one thing, they're all the same. Two eyes. One nose. One mouth. Colors of hair and skin can vary slightly, but you have to pay really close attention or you can easily confuse one Earthling for another.

Rebecca stared down at my empty tray. "Not eating?"

"Not hungry," I replied.

"Well, like, you don't even want like a chocolate chip cookie or something?"

"No thanks."

"Something to drink?" she asked. I could see this line of questioning might go on for a few eons, so I shrugged and said, "Why not?"

"I'll help you," said Rebecca.

Stuffing his third cream-filled sponge cake into his mouth, Gogol winked at me and said, "Why not?"

I followed Rebecca back into line. She pointed at an ancient-looking silver dispensary. "You like cola or root beer?"

"Whatever," I said in my best Earthling.

Rebecca shrugged and hit a button. Brown liquid filled a large paper vessel. Handing it to me, Rebecca said, "Take a sip. You'll like it. Although it's hard to believe they have no soda in Italy. Like, maybe I won't go there after all."

"Ahhh!" I said, my tentacles shaking with joy. Carbon dioxide! The magic fizz of life! Earthlings had it! Who would have guessed?

"More, please," I said, handing my vessel to Rebecca, then giving her ten more to fill up.

"Boy, you really are thirsty," said Rebecca. "Guess that's because you're so tall and stuff."

"Come on," yelled the Earthling behind us in

line. "You own stock in the company or something?"

Rebecca turned and gave him a cold stare. "Why don't you try acting like a human. Can't you see he's a guest?"

"From what planet?" said the Earthling.

"Very funny," said Rebecca. "You're just jealous because Rubi is so cool."

I'd just finished my seventh vessel of suspended $CO_2$ when another of those rude, piercing alarms split the air. It must have meant something to humans, because they all rose and began to move. As I stood, the $CO_2$ surged back up through my system and loudly released itself into the atmosphere. I felt much better. Gogol looked at me. "Where do you think Earthlings go when buzzers ring?"

I shrugged. "I have no idea. Let's follow Rebecca."

We went through a rectangular doorway into a square passageway lined with more rectangles. We entered one, and found ourselves in another square room. Gogol tapped me on the shoulder. "All these right angles are making me dizzy."

This square place had high ceilings with primitive light sticks attached that gave off a kind of slight, annoying buzz. At one end of the room was a black wall with chalky white hieroglyphic markings on it. Hanging near the door was a chart called a Periodic Table.

"Look, the Earthling alphabet," I whispered to Gogol. "We must be in a language class."

Rebecca sat down at a high rectangular table near the back of the room. As we joined her, her eyes grew wide with surprise.

"You guys have science this period?"

This was a science class? No way! Where was the Reverse-Molecular Ionization Chamber? Or the Cross-Visualization Test Module? They didn't even seem to have a Holographic Information Tub!

"I thought this was a language class," I said, pointing to the Periodic Table. "See, there's the alphabet."

"What's with Roma?" asked Rebecca. "Don't they teach you Italians anything? That's a Periodic Table. It lists all the known elements in the universe."

"But there's only one hundred and three!" Gogol said with a start.

"I know. That chart is ancient," replied Rebecca. "Mr. Forest says they've discovered at least three more elements in the last few years. But we have to make do with an old chart. School funding or something."

Gogol was wide-eyed. "But there are thousands of . . . ow! . . . Rubi, stop kicking me!"

"Me? Kick you? Must have been an accident. So, Rebecca, who is this Mr. Forest?"

Rebecca looked up as an older, male Earthling entered the room. "Him."

This guy was tall. Bigger than me. With huge, massive muscles. And a deep, rumbling voice.

"Today, class, we are going to continue our discussion about outer space. For starters, let's all pass our essays about the possibility of life on other planets to the front of the room." As he spoke, his two intense brown eyes swept over the classroom full of Earthlings. And came to rest on me.

# 12

## Arms Akimbo

Xela had begun to pace as I worked. Now she turned to me, her eyes flashing. "Arms, I don't care if getting help means expulsion. We've got to get them back! Now!"

"Look, Xela, I know I can figure this out if you'll just give me a minute."

"A minute on my planet or yours?"

"Whichever is longer."

"No way! A minute on your planet is five years on mine. We don't have that kind of time. I'm out of here."

Xela headed for the door. She had her hand around the knob and was pulling it open when she heard me scream.

"WAIT! I've got it! I've got it!"

Xela rushed back to the computer. "Are you sure this time?"

"Absolutely," I insisted. "I just forgot to align the Universal maxsis crom-dimmer with the rayn-forst control sim. How obvious can you get?"

"This better work, Arms!"

"Piece of cake. Like feeding candy to a ger-monger. With this hand I dial in the coordinates. This hand enters all crucial data. This hand pushes the activator, then, at just the right moment, the reclaim button. And this hand . . ."

"What?" asked Xela.

"With this hand I cross all six fingers."

"That's reassuring."

"Here we go!" Quick as a shimmer, I pushed three small buttons. The reclaim button began to glow. I took a breath and waited. It grew brighter. When it reached deep purple, I brought down one of my left hands, hard and fast, and punched it. The lights in the lab dimmed. I saw Xela cross her fingers.

# 13

## Rubidoux

Mr. Forest was on the move! Stomping down the aisle. Headed straight for me!

"Excuse me, young man, do you have a pass?"

"A pass?"

"A piece of paper. It has your name on it. They issue it in the office. You can't be in my class without it."

"Oh, that pass."

"It's okay, Mr. F. They're with me," said Rebecca.

"They?" asked Mr. Forest.

"This is Rubi. And this is Gogol. They're like exchange students form Rome. You know, in Italy. I'm showing them around."

"Not without a pass you're not. And young man, I suggest you take off that hat."

"Me?" I asked sheepishly.

"No, the alien behind you."

"But I'm not wearing a hat," Gogol just had to say.

Gogol is *so* dense. Just because he looks like an Earthling doesn't mean I'll be mistaken for one. I knew if I took off this piece of equipment Earthlings called a fedora, it would spell the end for me. I mean my skin was pretty much the same color as Mr. Forest's. And he was even taller than me. But purple tentacles?

As I reached up to do as I'd been commanded, I could feel my breath coming in short, little spurts. My skin started to tingle all over. My hearts were pounding wildly. Then, just as my fingers touched the brim, I heard Gogol say, "Mr. Forest, I'm not feeling so great. My skin feels all tingly. And my heart's beating wildly. I think I need to go lie down."

"I can take him to the nurse, Mr. Forest," Rebecca offered.

"I'm sure you can," said Mr. Forest. "And while you're at it, take Rubi to the office and see that he gets the proper pass."

All right, Gogol! Way to go. For once he saved me! But the tingling was getting worse! That's when

I noticed my fingers were beginning to disappear. The tingling wasn't nerves. It was Arms and Xela bringing us home! Just as we got outside the classroom door, Gogol dematerialized.

# 14

## Arms Akimbo

A rush of cold air filled the lab as the wormhole appeared. The computer hummed. The reclaim button began to flash.

"Here they come!" I yelled.

Xela held her breath and shut all three eyes. With a thud, something hit the floor, but Xela was too nervous to look.

"Gogol? Rubi? Is that you?" she asked.

"It's . . . it's . . . it's a book. *Our Changing Universe.*"

"But where are Rubi and Gogol?" Xela said, trembling.

All at once the wormhole twisted, groaned, and

pitched. "Stand back!" I hollered. "This is it!" Out of the wormhole flew dozens of papers. I ran to grab them.

"*Alone in the Universe,* by Maria Chavez. *Alien Life and Why It Doesn't Exist,* by Scott Levine. *My Brother Is a Teenage Alien,* by Rebecca Dahl. All marked, 'Mr. Forest's fifth period science class.' Is this some kind of a cosmic joke?"

"I don't know, Arms, but I'm going for help."

# 15

## Rubidoux

I could feel my molecules beginning to scatter as they prepared themselves for instantaneous intergalactic travel. Gogol wasn't the only one on his way back to Roma. Thank the six stars of Erin for Arms and Xela. And when I got back, I was going to kill Gogol. Forget that violence is forbidden by the Planetary Union. I'd just blame it on my exposure to Earthlings.

Except that something was wrong. Seriously wrong. When we rematerialized, we were still on Earth, standing next to Rebecca. Who just gave us a grin and said, "Cool!"

# 16

## Arms Akimbo

"Please, Xela, don't go. Let me give it just one more try. If it doesn't work this time, I promise I'll go with you for help."

"Cross your heart?"

I crossed my heart with my outside left hand.

"I want to see you cross with all four, or no deal."

"Okay, Xela. I've crossed with all four hands and twenty-four fingers. Do we have a deal?"

"One last try, and that's it."

"You'll thank me, Xela, when I get the them back and none of us is expelled."

"I'll just be happy we're out of The Tunnels breathing fresh orange air again."

"Then come help me. This is going to take both of us. I need one hand for the coordinates, one for the data, one to power up the locator, and—I think this was my big mistake last time—one hand needs to hold down the shift key. Then when I yell 'Punch it,' you hit the reclaim button."

Again I set the power level. Once more, I dialed in the coordinates for Planet RU1:2. Then, when everything was whirring and clanging and glowing, I yelled, "Punch it!"

Xela hit the reclaim button. There was . . . quiet. Absolute silence. Not even a sputter as the system crashed, plunging us into total darkness. Just as it did, the door to the lab flew open. In the harsh green light of The Tunnels, I could see a huge, hulking creature outlined in the doorway. Both of us froze as an angry voice shouted out, "HALT!"

# 17

## Rubidoux

I had to admit it. I should have paid more attention in Dead and Dying Worlds 101. Earth was a total mystery to me. I mean, we disappeared right in front of Rebecca's eyes and all she could say was "Cool?" She wasn't scared. She wasn't worried. She wasn't surprised. Could it be that Earthlings have mastered the art of instantaneous decomposition of matter? No way. These life forms are so primitive they still build everything using ninety-degree angles. Scary!

I did have another idea. As Rebecca walked next to me down the passageway, I took a quick brain scan. I thought it would be impossible to connect with her through my hat, but it was surprisingly easy. I was puzzled by what I found.

"Gogol," I whispered as we walked toward whatever an office is, "I don't know how to tell you this. Your ancestors have pretty large brains, but they only use about ten percent of them."

"Really?"

We both looked at Rebecca, who was busy telling us about who was cool at school and who wasn't. "So, what do they do with the rest of it?" Gogol wanted to know.

"Beats me," I admitted. "Packing material?"

"Here we are," Rebecca announced as she opened a door to a cavernous room. Naturally, it was another rectangle. It also had way too much light and a kind of sickly, sour smell. The room was empty. Maybe the smell had chased everyone away. I turned to Rebecca. "Is this where I get my pass?"

"No way," she answered. "Haven't you ever seen a gym before?"

"We met a Jim in the food line," offered Gogol.

"That was the boy, Jim. This is the room, gym. I've heard learning English is confusing. Guess it's really tough for Italians." Then, taking a deep breath of the poisonous-smelling air, Rebecca began to speak very, very slowly. "This. Is. A. Gym-na-si-um. No one has P.E. right now. We can hang out until next period. Follow me. We'll sit on the bleachers."

"I would like to ask you some questions about Earth," Gogol said as soon as we were bleached.

"Whatever. I'm no gardener, but I'll see what I can do."

"No, I mean the planet Earth."

"All I know is the sun comes up and the sun goes down. What else really matters?"

"Amazing," said Gogol. "The sun comes up?"

Rebecca rolled her eyes. "Like duh."

Gogol was out of his mind with excitement. "You know about DUH?" he cried.

"Huh?" said Rebecca.

I could see this was going nowhere fast. "Rebecca," I said, "why don't you tell us about some of your favorite places."

She looked at Gogol, then back at me. She took another breath of the sickly air. "Okay," she began, "so do you guys like malls?"

For the next thirty minutes we talked about Earth. Well, Rebecca talked. Gogol and I listened. And listened. And listened. I was amazed at an Earthling's ability to talk for a long time about nothing. If Earth ever does become part of the Planetary Union, this might help make them great diplomats.

Gogol kept trying to ask questions that had nothing to do with what Rebecca was talking about: What is the population of the planet? What is the distance from the sun? Is there intelligent life here? All Rebecca said was "Hey, you writing a book?"

Gogol smiled. "No. Just curious."

"Then why don't you go to the library? End of the hall, last door on the left. I'm sure Mrs. Hernandez can answer your questions. She's a real brain."

Gogol and I exchanged glances. Perhaps Rebecca's brain was not typical after all. "Thank you," Gogol said as he stood up. "I will go see the brain."

"Here, you'll need this."

"What is it?"

"A hall pass I keep for emergencies. Just give it back."

"Thank you," Gogol said. "Rubi, I'll meet you here later."

"Okay," I said, in spite of the fact that my tentacles were standing up and tingling. I knew we should probably stick together. But I could tell Rebecca didn't want me to go.

The loud, annoying buzzer sounded again. I'd learned by then they called it a bell. I didn't think I'd ever get used to such a horrible noise. But then I wasn't planning on being on Earth for long.

"Look, Rubi," Rebecca said, "I've got math last period. Why don't you wait here? I'll like meet you after class and we can take Gogol to the golden arches."

"Like, sure. Whatever." I was starting to get this Earth thing down.

Rebecca smiled. "Cool."

"Cool," I agreed. Was I good or what?

# 18

## Arms Akimbo

Even in the darkness I could see that whoever or whatever had screamed out HALT! was immense. Huge! Gigunda! Xela and I huddled together beneath the computer. "There's no way out," Xela whispered to me. "It's over."

I didn't answer. I couldn't. All I could do was to stare at the monster filling the doorway. "I know you are in here. Identify yourselves. Now!" The creature's webbed feet were pounding across the lab, causing the whole place to shake with tiny tremors. It was getting closer to us with every step it took.

I looked over at Xela. She'd shut all her eyes.

That's when I knew it was up to me. I figured, *It's dark. We're fast. If we can just get to The Tunnels, we can outrun this thing.* I nudged Xela and signaled for her to make a break for the door. With perfect timing, we burst out of our hiding place and flew past the monster. Only a few more steps and we'd be free! I put one arm out in front of me to push on the rock wall. With another I grabbed Xela's hand. Just one more step. . . . The lights came back on!

"I said halt!" The creature spun around and moved to cut off our escape. One of her fleshy arms reached out to grab us. Xela ducked. That's when the creature turned on me.

"Halt! Stop! Enough!" screamed the monster. But Xela wasn't stopping for anything. She reached out and pulled me toward the shelves. The creature followed. Her face twisted in anger. Two large blinking eyes perched at the end of stubby stalks narrowed in on us. "What are you doing here?" she said as she stomped closer and closer.

"Stay back!" yelled Xela in desperation. Frantically, we began grabbing artifacts off the shelves to defend ourselves with. As the creature lurched toward us, Xela picked up what looked like a very old stun gun. She took aim at the threatening life form. Then she hit the trigger. Immediately, a large parabolic shield shot out to protect us. "Saved!" yelled Xela with glee.

I heard Xela gasp as the creature pulled the shield from her hands and tossed it aside. There was nothing left to do but cringe. The creature was towering over us. Her enormous, hulking body blocked any form of escape. Then, in the very calmest voice, she asked, "Don't you know it's bad luck to open an umbrella indoors?"

"What?" I muttered, still in shock.

"An umbrella," said the creature. "It's a dangerous thing to open indoors."

Xela's whole body went limp as soon as she realized we weren't going to be attacked. Now she looked up at the creature and in a weak little voice asked, "What's an umbrella?"

"It is an item used on Planet RU1:2," the creature said. "But it seems to me, I'm the one who should be asking the questions. Would you mind sharing with me what you are doing here?"

"We don't mean any harm. Really. But you scared us," said Xela. "I'm Xela Zim Bareen and this is Arms Akimbo."

"Well, I'm Doctor Autonomou. And this is my lab. I'll look at my social calendar, but offhand, I don't recall inviting you here. In fact, I could swear The Tunnels are off-limits. Risk of expulsion, I believe. I think if you know what's good for you, you'll start explaining. Now!"

My heart had begun to settle down and my breathing was almost back to normal. Giving the creature my friendliest, don't-really-mean-any-harm smile, I began. "We're students. At DUH. And school sometimes, not all the time, you know, but sometimes, can get a little, kind of, sort of, well, boring, if you know what I mean."

"I'm waiting," said the creature. "And I'd appreciate it if you'd move to the punchline."

"We started exploring The Tunnels about three months ago. They're so incredible, we couldn't stay away. We stumbled on your lab last night," I blurted out all in one breath.

"I see. Adventurers," said Autonomou.

"Future diplomats," I told her with pride.

"At least we were going to be," Xela said sadly.

Autonomou scratched at one of her stalks. "I thought someone had been here, but decided it was impossible. My sense receptors had to be playing tricks on me. Guess I was wrong. Okay, so you found the lab last night. Why are you here now?"

"We came back to find out more about Planet RU1:2," Xela said.

"Really? Well, that is curious. There are not many left who have any interest in Earth."

"Earth!" gasped Xela.

"No wonder we can't get them back," I whispered.

# 19

## Gogol

I left Rubi with Rebecca and set out to find the library. That's when it started to happen. Everywhere I looked I saw things I *knew* I'd never seen before, yet they all seemed strangely familiar. I began to think this really might be home. Was that good or bad? I wasn't sure yet.

Making my way down the passageway Earthlings call a hall, I saw a door marked "Boys." It seemed odd to me that they would have one library for boys and one for girls. But I'd decided that with Earthlings anything was possible.

I pushed through the door. The room was dimly lit. Dank. The air felt heavy. There was a strange, unpleasant odor. I was hoping it wasn't the smell of bad information. In front of me, there were four very little rooms whose walls did not reach the ground. I could see someone's feet in the first one. They were obviously doing research. The only visible life form in the room was a man dressed all in brown. He was mopping the floor, which I took as a good sign. Most species know libraries are sacred and must be kept clean at all times, but from what I'd seen of Earth so far I hadn't expected such an advanced way of thinking.

"Excuse me," I asked the adult human. "Is this the boys' library?"

"It is if you brought your own reading material."

"I'm afraid I have nothing with me," I admitted. "Do I have to leave?"

The man smiled. "I was just joking. I think you made a wrong turn."

"That's a relief." I sighed.

"Well, this is the place for relief." Unsure what he meant, I stared at the man in confusion.

"Nevermind," he shrugged. "The library is down the hall, third door to the left." I opened the door to the hall just as the sound of rushing water filled the "Boys" room. I was lucky I got out of there in time.

Following the human's instructions, I found the library and entered. I sniffed the air, but there was no bad information odor. Perhaps I'd finally found the right place. I looked around. It was larger than the Boys' room, but smaller than the gym. Another rectangle filled with rectangles stacked on rectangles. Luckily, I was getting used to all the right angles. My dizziness had gone away.

The center of the room was dotted with, halellujah, round tables. A small group of Earthlings was seated at them, all looking as if they had been singled out for some kind of punishment. That made sense. Since humans can only use a tiny part of their brains, intaking too much information must be a form of torture.

At the front of the room sat the Library Master. On Roma, this is one of the highest positions any life form can be granted. I approached her with awe. "Excuse me," I said extra politely, "could you please direct me to the Holographic Information Tub? I wish to learn more about the planet."

The Library Master tilted her head down so she could look at me over the cornea correctors in front of her eyes. "Young man," she said sternly, "do you have a hall pass?"

"Yes, I do!" I said excitedly. Then I pulled the slip of paper Rebecca had given me from my pocket and showed it to her.

"Very well," she said, still none too friendly. "But I'm afraid our 'Holographic Information Tub' is on the fritz right now. Luckily our books are all in working order. Can I help you find something?"

"I want to learn all I can about Earth."

"Well now, that's refreshing," she said, smiling for the first time. "Why don't you start over there in the reference section? Biographies and nonfiction are also along that wall. Does that help?"

"Yes, thank you. When will your H.I.T. unit be operational again?"

"Ohhh, could be a long time," she whispered in a confidential tone of voice. "Who knows, I may decide to replace it with a refrigerator instead."

"Oh, I see," I said, nodding my head. *What a fascinating discovery,* I thought as I made my way to the books. *Earthlings like their information cold.*

I decided to start at the very beginning and make my way through the shelves. I picked up the first book. Its title was "A." I have to admit. I was so excited I began to tremble as I read. Almost from birth, Alzorian children are taught to read quickly and to memorize each passage. I was thankful now for my earlier training. I had a whole library to get through before half an ikron was up. I quickly made my way through the section marked "Reference" and moved on to the shelves termed "Biography." I was halfway through the C's when I heard someone clear their throat. I looked up to see the Library Master. "Young man, may I ask what you are doing?"

"You may," I answered with a smile.

"Well, gee, thank you," she said sounding less than pleased. "So what are you doing?"

"I am reading all about Earth," I answered.

"And as you complete each one you put it on the floor so you know you've finished it. Correct?"

Rebecca was right. The Library Master was a brain. "Exactly!" I said.

"Excuse me, young man. But no one can read this fast. It seems to me you are more intent on taking everything off the shelves than in reading."

"Would you like me to read more slowly?" I asked politely.

The Library Master turned red. "No. You go right ahead. What did you say your name was?"

"I am Gogol."

"Is that your first name or last?"

I had to think about that one. Was it a trick question? "Both," I said finally. "It is the first name I was given and I expect it will be the last." She got me to wondering if Earthlings were in the habit of changing their names every so often. That would be really confusing.

"Okay," she said. "Just stay right here. We'll see what the principal has to say about the mess you've made."

# 20

## Arms Akimbo

Autonomou stood over me, glaring. "Get who back?" she demanded. "What are you talking about?"

Xela and I looked at each other. I spoke first. "Nothing, really. I was just saying it was time for us to get back. It's been so nice meeting you."

I grabbed Xela and headed for the door. Xela looked over her shoulder. "Bye," she said with a smile.

"Yeah, bye," I said. "Maybe we'll see you around. Do you teach any classes? We'd love to take one. Sorry we can't stay and chat."

As I talked I just kept moving, pulling Xela with

me. The Tunnels were only steps away. We were just about to cross the threshold when the door slammed shut. I threw my weight against it. Locked!

Autonomou's voice shook with anger. "You two are not leaving until you tell me the truth. And remember, my species lives for hundreds of years. I've got plenty of time. Now, would you like to tell me what's going on here?"

Xela turned to me. Her yellow pupils had turned dark gold—a sign that she was really worried. "Arms, we have to tell her," she pleaded. "Autonomou can help us."

I felt desperate. "No!" I tried to reason. "She'll turn us in. We'll get kicked out of school. Maybe we could . . . I mean, what if . . ." I couldn't go on. I knew Xela was right. If we ever hoped to see Rubi and Gogol again we had no choice.

"Well? I'm waiting," said Autonomou.

"Our friends are in trouble," Xela began. "And we hope you can help us."

"Then you are going to have to tell me everything that happened. From the beginning." Autonomou stared long and hard at me. "Starting now, young lady!"

My voice came out so low I could see Autonomou straining to hear me. I couldn't help it. I was practically choking on the lump in my throat. "Last night we saw a creature from RU1:2 on your screen. It looked like someone we know at DUH, someone who thinks he is totally unique in the universe."

"You must be referring to Gogol," Autonomou said.

"You know him?" Xela exclaimed.

"Not exactly. I know him by sight. I've observed him from a distance. And I have reviewed his file. His appearance is quite curious, really."

"Exactly. So you can understand why we brought Gogol here tonight to show him what we'd found," I said.

"Oh, no. I think I can see where this is headed," groaned Autonomou. She set her large frame down into a low-slung chair. It sighed under her weight.

"I was trying to pull up more data when an alarm went off."

Autonomou smiled. "The one I set."

"We were all running out when Gogol . . ."

"Found another way out?"

"That's one way to put it," said Xela. "He picked up the WAT-Man that was here on your work-bench, entered the coordinates for RU1:2, and jumped into a wormhole."

"We had no idea it was Earth," I said.

"This is worse than I thought. That WAT-Man was only partway through its test cycle," exclaimed Autonomou.

"Our friend Rubidoux tried to stop him, but

ended up falling in with him. And that's the story," I said, hanging my head.

Autonomou was quiet for several seconds. Finally she stood up. The two purple veins on each side of her head throbbed. She looked really upset. When she began to speak, the words came out slowly, as if they were almost too painful to say. "Do you know what you have done? Lives are at stake here. And not just your friends'. Hundreds of others', as well. If news of this gets out, you will have destroyed all my efforts to make contact with Earth. Two hundred years of struggle, work, and hope. For nothing."

Autonomou was pacing now. "The wormhole to Earth is not stable. It collapses. Spins out of control. Shows up late, or not at all. I have been able to open and close it randomly for years. That's where all these artifacts came from. But it's not stable enough for life forms to travel through it. With luck, I may be able to do that in another fifty years."

Xela looked horrified. "That long?"

"With luck," said Autonomou. "So you can see how I feel about your two friends deciding to pay a little visit to Earth."

"One decided. The other tried to stop him," I corrected.

Autonomou waved my words away. "No matter. They have now both joined the ranks of other diplomats who are stranded on RU1:2."

"Stranded?" I choked. "What others?"

"Dr. Autonomou," said Xela. "I don't know who's stranded where, but we *have* to get our friends back."

Autonomou turned away. "I'm sorry," she said. "I don't know if that will be possible."

"We have to try," Xela said firmly.

Autonomou put an arm around each of us. "We'll do that," she said. "But there's something you both need to understand. It is possible you may never see your friends again."

# 21

## Gogol

I watched the Library Master walk to the front of the room. "I'd like your attention, please," she said sternly. "I will be out of the room for just a few minutes. While I am gone, I expect you to act like the adults you claim to be. Remain in your seats. No talking. No nonsense. Lea, I'm leaving you in charge."

The Library Master let her eyes sweep the room. They locked in on a tall, freckle-faced human in the back of the room. "Got that, William?"

"Yes, Mrs. Hernandez."

"Good. Anyone caught disobeying will have morning detention." She gave one last, sharp look around the room, then turned to go out the door. As she walked away, I strained to see the base of her neck. I was anxious to know if something I'd read about Earthlings was true. But her neck was covered by hair.

There was, however, something on Mrs. Hernandez's back. An identification tag of some sort? Whatever it was, it must have been funny, because the kids all started to shake with muted laughter. I strained to read it, decoding it just as she stepped out the door. "Kiss me!" it said.

The second the door slammed, the Earthlings began to disobey their orders. Some got up. Others slouched down. All of them were talking. Several of them were looking at me and pointing.

"Hey, kid! Come here," one of them called out.

Curious as to the Earthling thought process, I crossed the room to where the one who had called me sat. An enormous grin was plastered on his face. On Roma, those who know me think I'm pretty clever. I put it to work now, relying on the Earthling speech I'd picked up from Rebecca to pull me through. "Like, how about that Mrs. Hernandez? What a dork. She's so lonely she has to advertise for a kiss. Talk about gross."

But no one answered. They just looked at me with blank expressions. Then they looked at each other. And began to snicker.

"I put that on her back, you dweeb," said the

one Mrs. Hernandez had called William. "Are you for real?"

"Not only am I real," I reminded him, "but my mind is functioning at ninety-nine percent efficiency. That is, by the way, ten times your brain function."

William sneered. "Oh, gee. What a put-down," he said, shaking with mock fear. "And what's with the fashion statement, dude? Pick them up at a garage sale in another galaxy?" I wasn't sure quite what to say. But it was becoming increasingly clear why Earth was not part of the Union. There was a lot of unnecessary hostility here.

"Lay off the new kid, Willy," someone said. That cheered me up. Maybe there was hope for the planet after all.

"Okay, okay, Lea. I was just having a little fun. Here, no hard feelings, right pal?" The William-type human extended his hand. Luckily, I'd seen others perform this custom before. Smiling, I raised my hand to meet his. But just as I was about to grab his, he pulled it away, leaving mine floating in midair. "I guess Mr. Ninety-nine percent has a little bit left to learn, huh?" William said as he slapped me on the back. Then he walked away.

And there it was. What I'd been looking for. Above William's collar and below his hairline there was . . . nothing. Just the same smooth skin that seemed to cover all of an Earthling's body. In a trance I lifted my hand and touched the back of my own neck. The thick reptilian skin that ran from the base of my skull to the base of my spine felt hard, rough, and . . . alien. In that instant I knew the truth. I was a mutant. Part Alzorian, like my parents, part Earthling. At this particular moment in time, I was glad the Alzorian part of me was covered by my clothing and the hair on my head. If William was at all typical, it was clear that Earthlings wouldn't think too highly of aliens.

My thoughts were interrupted by loud hooting sounds. I looked up to see that some of the humans had gathered over by where I'd been reading earlier. "Hey, get a load of this!" one of them called to the others.

I walked over and was immediately bombarded with questions.

"Man, what were you thinking?"

"No wonder Hernandez is mad."

"Why did you pull all these books down?"

"I was reading," I answered.

"Yeah, right."

The one named Lea came up and stood by me. "Hey, maybe he's a speed reader." The rest of them shook their heads and mumbled a round of whatevers, then moved off in different directions.

"So how fast can you read?" asked Lea.

"I don't know," I admitted. "I've never checked. Do you want to time me?"

"Sure," she agreed, pulling a book from the shelf.

"Here, take this book. It's a biography of George Washington Carver and it's 210 pages long. I'll watch the clock and tell you when to go."

I took the book from her. "This will be fun. I advise you not to blink."

Lea smiled as she watched the clock. "Okay. Get ready. Get set. Go!"

I opened the book and flipped through the pages. It didn't take long. "Done," I announced, banging it shut.

"That was only like five seconds. Here, give me the book. I'll quiz you."

"You don't believe me?"

"Let's just say I think you could be pulling my leg," she said, and smiled.

That puzzled me. If I was pulling her leg, how could she still be standing? And what did leg pulling have to do with believing someone? I was beginning to wish Rebecca were here. She was easier to understand.

Lea opened the book and scanned a page. "Okay," she began. "What did George Washington Carver's father do?"

"He was a slave."

"Okay, that was an easy one," she said turning a chunk of pages. "What college did Carver go to?"

"Simpson College in Iowa. That's on page 103."

"Oh, I get it," Lea said with a laugh. "You've read this before. Fess up!"

"No, I swear on the six stars of Erin."

"What?" asked Lea.

"Never mind. Here, let's try another," I said reaching for a book called *Thomas Jefferson*. Just then, the door from the hall burst open. Framed in the doorway was a large male Earthling with a shiny skull. He glanced quickly around the room, then yelled, "Okay. That's enough."

The Earthlings scampered back to their seats. Within seconds, they had assumed the pose of model students. But the hairless Earthling and Mrs. Hernandez had no interest in them. They were headed straight for me!

"Look, Mr. Moore! He's at it again," Mrs. Hernandez said as she pointed at the mound of books piled around me on the floor. "He pulled all these books down. Says he's a new student. I'd like to know where they teach manners like that."

The hairless one looked down at the pile of books. Then up at me. "Son, what's going on here? We have no new students starting today."

Thinking fast, I remembered the slip of paper in my pocket. "Here," I said, "perhaps this will explain." The Earthling scrunched up his forehead as he studied the pass Rebecca had given me.

"This tells me a lot," he said, turning it over and over in his hand.

Saved! At least for now. But I vowed that as soon as I got away from the library I was going to find

Rubi and get back to Roma. Stuffing the pass into his pocket, the Moore-type human put his face right up to mine. "It tells me that you have a phony hall pass. And that you have no business here. I suggest you follow me to the office so we can get this straightened out."

With that, Mr. Moore took me by the elbow and steered me toward the door. Suddenly, he came to a halt. I could feel his eyes on my back. "It's a skin condition," I said quietly.

Mr. Moore gave my shirt a tug. "No, it's a prank," he said holding up a piece of paper with the words "Kick Me" scrawled across it. Mr. Moore looked around the room. "We'll take care of this later." William's annoying laugh was the last thing I heard as I was led out of the room.

# 22

## Xela Zim Bareen

Arms and I fell silent as Doctor Autonomou took her place at the computer controls. The lab felt unbearably hot to me. My breath was coming in short little rattles. The room seemed to buckle and sway.

Autonomou didn't even break concentration. She just ordered me to take a deep breath. Then she added more gently, "I know how brave you two are. I'm counting on that. Now let's see what the three of us can do." Then she went back to checking the data on the screen. "Arms, was it you who set up these equations for the target tracking system?"

"Uh-huh, did I mess it up?"

"To the contrary, you did an excellent job. Quite the scientist, I'd say."

"She reads a lot," I offered.

Arms blushed. "It's no big deal. How long do you think it will take to get everything back on-line?"

"We'll have to wait several minutes for the Think-U-Bators to cool down and for the rayn-forst sims to warm up. After that, I'll have to re-enter some of the data." Autonomou looked thoughtful. "I'd say another half ikron or so. This isn't like the systems on the surface. It's been patched together from whatever discarded pieces of equipment I've been able to find. It may not look like much, but I've done the best I could under the circumstances."

"Doctor, I don't want to seem impolite, but exactly what are the circumstances?" I asked. "I mean, a secret lab hidden in the furthest, most remote part of The Tunnels. A system put together from equipment so old you'd have to search to find it on the Holographic Information Tub. A brilliant scientist who isn't teaching at the school, but spends her time investigating things like umbrellas. I don't get it. What's going on?"

Autonomou turned her gaze on me. If she was angry, I couldn't tell. I'd never talked to an adult like that before. But then, I'd never had two friends mailed across the galaxy before, either.

After staring at me for what felt like an eternity, Autonomou let out a deep sigh. "I never thought

I'd tell the whole story to anyone. It's a secret I've kept for two hundred years. But you've already seen the lab. You know about RU1:2. In a way, it will be a relief to finally share it. But before I go any further, I have to swear you to secrecy. Reputations, even lives, depend on this remaining a secret."

Arms shot me a look that said, Do we really want to know this? But then we shook our heads, and said, "By Erin."

Autonomou got up and started pacing the lab. "What do they teach you about Earth these days?"

"Not much," said Arms. "Least known of the lesser planets. A world so war-torn and violent that it's considered hopeless by the PU's High Council."

"The High C has even put out an Eternal Ban on all travel to Earth," I added.

"What's always seemed weird to me," said Arms, "is that there are only a few known images of Earth. A mushroom cloud. A Class Seven star lighting up a barren, frozen wasteland. Toppled statues broken into a thousand pieces. Bombed-out landscapes. There's nothing growing. Nothing pretty. And strangest of all, no pictures of the creatures who live there."

"They either blend into their surroundings really well or their molecular structure makes them invisible to image capture," I said.

Autonomou shook her head. She let out a long, low chuckle. But the look on her face was of pure sadness. "Would it shock you to find out it's all lies? Everything you know about Earth, everything you've been told, is a complete fabrication designed to keep you and future generations from learning the truth."

Arms and I looked at each other. The idea that all the professors at DUH would lie to the students was too fantastic to believe. From our very first days at DUH, all students were taught that lying is against the Code of Values. Without strict devotion to the Code there could be no Planetary Union. It's the glue that holds all life forms in the Union together peacefully. Okay. Occasionally someone is caught lying. But when it's discovered, it's firmly dealt with. Listening to Autonomou, it seemed to me there was only one logical explanation: We were in the presence of a nut. A brilliant nut, but a nut all the same. I looked straight at the eyes at the end of Autonomou's stalks. "What are you saying? That all the professors at DUH are involved in a cover-up about Earth?"

"Not all of them," answered Autonomou. "Only the ones who have been around for the last two hundred years." It must have been obvious to Autonomou that we were having trouble believing her. "Let me explain," she said. "Here, sit down."

Arms sat on the chair at the computer. I took a seat at the workbench. Autonomou continued to pace as she spoke. "To understand, you must take

100

yourself back to the glory days of DUH. Mission specialists were being sent to far-flung worlds at a record pace. There were only 124 planets in the Union then. Alzor, Krynon and Penx have since been added. It was such an exciting time. It felt like overnight we went from a primitive understanding of wormhole travel to such wide acceptance that high-placed individuals were even allowed to summon a wormhole for something as casual as a trip across town."

"Everyone does that now," I said, unimpressed.

"I know," said Autonomou, "and it's totally irresponsible. Anyway, as you know, Roma was chosen as the site for diplomatic headquarters because it lies at the crossroads of a great many wormholes."

"All intergalactic highways lead to Roma," said Arms, reciting the school motto.

"Quite right. And most of them are well-traveled trade routes and highways. But not all wormholes are stable. After all, they are a force of nature. Our ability to control them is limited. Anyway, about two hundred years ago . . ."

Suddenly, Autonomou broke off her story. A sadness hung in the air. I was afraid to move. The lab was completely silent. Then, as quickly as she had gone quiet, Autonomou seemed to shake off the mood. "Anyway," she continued, "I was both a professor at DUH and a scientist whose specialty was wormholes. In fact, many of my discoveries made intergalactic travel possible."

"That's where I know your name from," I interrupted. "I've been trying to place it all night. You're the Autonomou who's credited with the Theory of Symbiotic Attraction. You did the early work on wormhole strengthening."

It was Arms's turn to be impressed. "Xela, we don't study wormhole theory until the advanced grades. How do you know that?"

"Hey, I read too," I said with a laugh. Then I turned my gaze on Autonomou. Something just wasn't adding up. "But the books say your experiments failed."

"Yes, I know what they say. You will also note they say I am dead. But they are wrong on both counts."

"So what happened?" Arms asked.

"It's simple, really," Autonomou said wistfully. "I was highly successful at stabilizing the more commonplace wormholes. The ones everyone uses every day now—even to go shopping, of all things. But what intrigued me, what I wanted to do most was lock in the unreliable wormholes. The ones that buckle and spin out of control for no reason. I accomplished this. In the lab, at least. My assistants and I tested my theories over and over and over. I was hailed as a genius. A title I felt I richly deserved. Unfortunately, my pride blinded me to the dangers."

"What's all this got to do with Earth?" Arms sighed.

"Patience!" snapped the doctor.

"Sorry," Arms said quickly.

"When I felt we were ready to test my theories outside of the laboratory, we looked for a wormhole that would fit all the necessary requirements. After considering several sites, we finally settled on the one to Earth. It was perfect for our experimental purposes. But there was one problem."

"The wormhole collapsed whenever it was summoned?" asked Arms.

"If only it had been that simple," said the doctor. "Earthlings were the trouble. As you know, the Planetary Union only sends missions to planets where they feel there is some hope of change occurring, where peace will become a way of life. The High Council felt Earthlings could not be helped. They would never be reformed, no matter how many missions we sent there. And so they denied permission to try and link with Earth.

"That's when I made my crucial mistake. Instead of accepting the High Council's order, I pleaded with them to change their minds. I'd been studying Earth for quite some time before suggesting it. I felt there was reason to believe its beings could change. True, they seemed to love violence. Wars were commonplace. But then, too, they'd produced the music of Bach and The Beatles. The art of Michelangelo. The poems of Dr. Seuss. In my heart of hearts, I knew Earth was worth the risk. I successfully argued my case to the High Council. For the first time ever, they changed a ruling to support the opinion of a scientist."

Autonomou stopped pacing and sat down. She looked each of us directly in the eyes. "The experiment was successful. We began to send mission specialists, 175 in all, through the stabilized wormhole. As was typical in these kind of missions, they were spread throughout Earth's history and across its land mass. All specialists had one common goal. Mingle with the local population, gain their trust, and teach them the ways of peace. Then get out."

"What happened?" I asked quietly. Autonomou turned away. Her voice became so quiet I could hardly hear what she was saying. "One year to the day after we sent the first diplomat down, all contact was lost. Our diplomats were stranded. Goners."

"Goners?"

"No one knew for certain what happened. The High Council was convinced Earth's violence had infected the diplomats. Worried Earth's evil ways would spread back up the wormhole like a disease, they ordered the connection smashed."

"What?" cried Arms.

"What if they were wrong?" I said. "What if it

was just the wormhole collapsing? That would mean they left 175 mission specialists behind to be discovered and destroyed."

"Exactly," agreed Autonomou. "That's what I believed. But I was pulled off the project. Disgraced. Ridiculed. The High Council felt what they had done was for the greater good. But they also took pains to hide it. My discoveries were erased from the textbooks. I lost my funding. My lab. My reputation. I was no longer allowed to teach at DUH. They proclaimed the mission to Earth a lost cause and locked away all information about it. Earth was declared a "Dying Planet." It became forbidden to talk about it in any other way. All travel there was banned. The Council did not want future generations of diplomats to question the safety of their own missions or the wisdom of the Council."

The wounds ran deep in Autonomou. I could feel it. But there was something that didn't make sense. "Yet, here you are. Working in this cave of a lab."

"I am here in secret," Autonomou confided. "I rescued the database, at least what I could. But my information is woefully incomplete. I managed to build this lab from surplus equipment. For the past two hundred years, my life has been dedicated to getting those diplomats back. But now I'm 476 years old. I don't have much time left."

"I don't get it," said Arms. "How could you be

down here for all these years without anyone knowing?"

"I can't tell you that. Let's just say I have friends in high places," Autonomou said mysteriously.

"But you've succeeded! The wormhole to Earth is working," I pointed out.

"Yes, it works. Most of the time. But all I've been able to pull through it are the artifacts you see here. Loose change, socks, keys, wallets, contact lenses, directions . . ."

"Homework," Arms added.

"Yes, quite a bit of homework, it seems. But the system needs much more testing before sending life forms through it."

I looked away, but Autonomou seemed to know what I was thinking. "But there's no time for that now. We'll have to do the best we can with what we have."

Suddenly the voice of the computer rang out, startling me. "Systems maximized," it announced.

"Time to get busy," said Autonomou as she took her place at the console.

# 23

## Arms Akimbo

I might have a reputation as a whiz at the computer, but it was amazing to watch Autonomou work. She was *quick*. So sure of herself. I didn't want to admit it, but it was a big relief to have her at the controls. "Universal maxsis crom-dimmer. On. Rayn-forst control sim. Aligned. Think-U-Bators. On-line." Her words were music to my ears.

"Is there anything we can do to help?" asked Xela.

"I don't think so. I've been operating this system so long, I know exactly what I need to do. It would take longer to try and explain it. And with the suns about to rise on the surface, I'm sure you two would like to get this over with as soon as possible."

"That's for sure," said Xela. "If we're not back in the dorms before the suns come up, we'll be retro-fitting Scrapebotz for infinity."

That brought me back to reality. I took Xela's hand in all of mine. "Look, Xela. You should go back now."

Naturally, Xela started to protest, but I knew this time I was right. "There's no reason for all of us to get in trouble. You're the one with the most to lose. You're at the head of your class. You've already been selected for mission specialist school. Half of DUH would give their lives for that honor. You can't let it slip away."

Xela turned toward me. A cold look was in her eyes. I had no idea what she was thinking. "Arms Akimbo. Every night for three months we've been coming to these tunnels. We could have been caught. Sent home. Had our lives ruined forever. Whatever rules we hadn't broken before, we destroyed completely when we brought Gogol here. Now our friends really need us. And if you think I'm going to let you stay down here alone . . ."

I held my breath. I knew these words. I'd said them to Rubi only the day before. Now Xela put her face right up to mine. "You're wrong!" she exclaimed.

I started to tell her I totally understood. I mean Xela was brave, but . . . then her words sunk in. "You're staying? Well, rockin' Roma-rama!" I yelled. I was so happy I wrapped Xela in a four-arm, full-press hug and squeezed.

"Arms! Arms! Please! I can't breathe," gasped Xela.

I laughed and stood back. "Sorry. I got just a teensy bit excited."

"It's one for all and all for one and don't you ever forget that," said Xela. Then she turned back to see what was happening on the computer screen. That's when I noticed it. The third eye at the back of Xela's head. Its light had begun to shine again.

"You got it, Xela," I said, smiling.

# 24

## Rubidoux

Rebecca and Gogol hadn't been gone long when other Earthlings began entering the gym. This group looked sort of like the other Earthlings we'd seen, but something was a little off. For one thing, only the male of the species appeared. For another, they all had a kind of sad uniform on. Big and baggy. Grayish white shirts over red, embarrassingly short pants. These exposed knobby discs covering their knees. Strange. And, well, ugly too. As this group of males ran out to the middle of the room, their shoes squeaked as if they were alive and in pain. It was an awful thing to have to hear.

Then one of these humans started bouncing a rubbery sphere. True to Earth's reputation for violence, he kept hitting the floor with it. All the others clearly wanted this sphere for themselves. But the first human ran around with it, twisting and turning away from the others. He was not about to give it up. Finally, the others started screaming at him, holding their arms up in the air and jumping up and down. This must have made him afraid, because he suddenly heaved the sphere up in the air. Like malls, calves, and the golden arches, this sphere must have some kind of important meaning to Earthlings because everyone was trying to touch it as it came down.

"Hey, you!" I heard a voice yell out. I was glad I wasn't U. This guy sounded mad.

"I'm talking to you! Turn around and face me!" Not sure who this Earthling was speaking to, I turned around to help him look for U.

"That's better," said a thin adult with a clipboard.

Wanting to help him with his confusion, all I could say was, "But I'm not U."

"A wise guy, huh?" he said glaring up at me.

"Well, I use more than ten percent, if that's what you mean."

"We'll deal with that another time," he said. "For now, just tell me why you're here."

"It's all Gogol's fault."

"Okay," he said, turning an interesting shade of

red, "we'll try this again. Where did you come from?"

My back tentacle began to dance and the words, "Science class," popped out of my mouth.

The thin man looked relieved. "Now we're making some progress. I've never seen you before, so I take it you are a new student." As he talked he walked in a circle around me and I could see he was admiring my great Douxwhopian height. "I'm Assistant Coach Ned Bean." Then holding up the sphere he asked, "Ever play basketball?"

"Not that I know of."

"Really? Stay right here," said Coach Bean. He ran across the gym floor, his shoes yelping in agony, and went through a door. Seconds later he came out with a shorter, well-stuffed Earthling. Coach Bean pointed to me from across the room. The other man's eyes grew wide.

"You. Over here. On the double," yelled Assistant Coach Bean. I don't know what gave him the idea that he had any authority over me, but I figured it was best to play along. All the other kids in the gym watched as I ran across the middle of the floor. It was probably because my shoes weren't screaming.

"This is Head Coach Struthers. He . . ."

"Clam up, Bean. I'll take it from here," snapped the coach. He looked me over, toes to tentacles. At six feet six inches tall, I was a full head taller than him.

"So you want to try out for my team, huh?" he finally said.

"I do?" I asked.

"Yes, you do," said Bean, nodding furiously.

"Well, not in those shoes, buster," Struthers snarled.

"Whatever," I said cheerfully and turned to go back to the other side of the gym. I had no interest in anything that involved torturing shoes.

"Wait!" cried Bean. I stopped and listened as Assistant Coach Bean appealed to his superior.

"Sir." Bean dropped his head as he spoke. "Consider the possibilities here. This could be a great break for us. If this guy's any good, we'll have a shot at the state championship."

I could see Bean was making headway.

"And you know what that means. Your name in the paper, TV interviews, sponsors lining up to give money . . ."

You could almost see Coach Struthers's neural network light up. "I'll get to go to the coaches' clinic in Orlando next winter?"

"Yep," said Bean. I was now wondering who was really in charge. "And with the money that's left you can get that desk chair that swivels."

That did it.

"Kid," Coach Struthers called out, "the shoes can stay, but the hat has to go."

I hesitated. I felt I'd be in danger if I didn't join in

this basketball ritual. But I was worried my purple tentacles would be too much for them. Coach Bean seemed to read my thoughts.

"Don't worry, kid. Hair like that will make you a star in the NBA."

"Whatever," I said as I removed my hat. I could feel the eyes of everyone in the room as they stared at the tentacles that covered my head. The tentacles resemble hair, except that they are thicker and sort of fleshy. Coach Struthers cut the stares short by blowing hard into a small silver gadget.

"All right, listen up," he called out. "This is, hey . . . what's your name?"

"Rubi."

"Okay," the Coach continued. "This is Rudy and he's new."

"Excuse me, Coach Struthers," I interrupted. "It's Rubi, not Rudy."

"Ruby? Like R-U-B-Y? Ruby?"

"Sure," I agreed.

"Okay. Fine." He turned back to the students. "My mistake. This is 'Ruby.' "

The Earthlings snickered. Someone called out, "Is it a boy or a girl?"

Coach Struthers stepped up. "That's enough. He wants to try out for basketball, so we're going to have a little scrimmage, got it?"

The group fell silent and nodded.

"Good. Now, spread out."

Coach Bean slapped me on the back, "Okay, Ruby. Give it all you got."

There was a sudden surge of energy in the room. The male Earthlings came alive. I watched for a few seconds as they ran around, bounced the ball, passed it, and then tried to toss it through one of two hoops only slightly larger than the ball itself.

"Hey, Ruby, catch the ball!" yelled a dark-haired specimen.

I grabbed the sphere out of midair and gave it a bounce. My long fingers fit its curve perfectly. Another Earthling ran up to me.

"What are you going to do with that ball, stretch?" a voice sneered. It was Red, of course. My tentacles quivered. With my hat off, it was pretty easy to read his thoughts. "So you want to take the ball away from me?" I said. "Think you can get in it in that little hoop? Well, here's news. You've got nothing on me. Or anyone else in the galaxy. You're working with only eight percent."

"Ruby, over here! Over here!" yelled some of the other Earthlings. But another human had joined Red. They had me surrounded. I couldn't move. I could have passed it, but instead I took aim at the hoop at the other end of the court. I lifted my arms, flicked my wrist, and propelled the ball in that direction. Everyone turned to watch. The ball curved through the air. It hit the rim, then bounced straight up. And came down through the middle of the hoop.

The gym fell quiet.

"I'm sorry I hit the rim," I said to no one in particular. "Does it count anyway?"

"Yeah. For my team," Red snickered. "You put it in the wrong basket, dork."

"That's okay, that's okay, Ruby," shouted Coach Bean, clapping his hands. "That was one heck of a shot, son. One heck of a shot!"

Coach Struthers was grinning from ear to ear. I checked into his thoughts. He was already planning what he would say on TV when his team won the state championship. "A good team starts with good coaching," it began.

# 25

## Arms Akimbo

Autonomou pushed herself away from the console. "We're nearly ready," she announced, "except for one thing." Then she crossed the room to the workbench and began to rummage through the clumps of wires and gear.

"I couldn't find anything useful over there," said Xela. "Gogol took the WAT-Man with him."

"I know," said the doctor, "but you probably weren't looking for this." Autonomou turned toward us. In the palm of her hand rested a small box. It was deep purple in color with a small red insignia on it.

This puzzled me. "That mark looks like the one used by the Technology Optimize Program."

**117**

"What's that?" asked Xela.

"TOP labs is the Union's number one research center," I revealed. "It's where most of the latest stuff comes from. And, like the name says, everything done there is *very* top secret!"

"Very good, Arms," said Autonomou. "Again, you seem to have done your homework. This is indeed the TOP mark." Autonomou began to open the box. "What's in this box will, I hope, help us get your friends home." Xela and I watched in awe as a soft, golden light filled the lab.

Then Autonomou pulled out a small, glowing crystal pyramid. Carefully, she held it up and examined it. "This is a High Cram Cranium Crystal. It is the absolute latest in computer science. It's so tightly packed with information and processing power, it's designed to be the last upgrade anyone will ever need."

"I've heard that before," I said.

"Yes, but this is truly different. The micro-circuits in the crystal are designed to make copies of themselves as your need for power increases. The more you use this crystal, the more information it's able to store. Here, you hold it."

I put out my upper right hand. The crystal was surprisingly light, but it tingled like it was vibrating. I couldn't take my eyes off of it.

"How did you get this?" I asked. "Only three are known to exist."

"That's not important right now," said Autonomou as she took the crystal back. "As I said, I have friends in high places. What is important is that we get your fellow adventurers back."

Autonomou sat back down at the computer and set the crystal on the top of the control panel.

"Aren't you going to hook it up?" asked Xela.

"No need. The crystal just has to be near the computer to work. All right. Let's give this a try. I've only had the crystal a few days. It does seem to help shore up the wormhole, but I've never used it in a live experiment before. This seems as good a time as any."

"Experiment?" I said. "That sounds kind of, you know, a little, you know, uncertain maybe . . ."

"Experiment," replied Autonomou. "But it's our best, maybe our only, chance for getting them back."

Nothing more was said as Autonomou got to work. The glow from the High Cram Cranium Crystal pulsed once and then spread out over the computer console. A brilliant light filled the lab. Strange shadows danced across the walls and ceiling.

Autonomou waved for Xela and me to join her. "I'm going to need your help. I've already aligned the maxsis crom-dimmer with the rayn-forst control sim, dialed in the coordinates, and entered all the crucial data. All that's left . . ."

"I know," I said. "One of us has to power up the

locator, hold down the shift key, and then when you yell, 'Punch it,' hit the reclaim button."

"I can see you've done this before, Arms," said Autonomou.

"Too many times tonight," I told her.

"Dr. Autonomou, I think you should have the honor of hitting reclaim," said Xela. "After all these years, you should be the first one to bring a life form back from Earth."

Autonomou smiled. "Thank you, Xela." Then she turned her head away and cleared her throat. In a husky voice she asked, "Is everyone ready?"

"What should I do?" asked Xela.

"Cross your fingers," said Autonomou.

"The locator is ready, Doctor, and the shift key is down."

"Punch it!" yelled Xela.

Autonomou's trembling finger hovered above the reclaim button for a moment. She closed her eyes. Then pressed it.

"Reclaim on auto-pause," the computer announced.

"What's going on?" I asked.

Autonomou eyed the data on the computer screen and groaned. "I have good news and bad news," she said. "The good news is that the crystal is doing its job. We have a firm grip on the wormhole to Earth. The bad news is that the wormhole cuts right through a space storm."

"A what?" asked Xela.

"A space storm. Strong solar winds along with radiation showers, heavy at times, are hitting the greater Earth area. The wormhole is tossing and twisting. It's rock solid at this end. But the other end is flapping in the breeze."

"What do we do?" I asked in panic.

"Nothing we can do, really," sighed Autonomou. "We'll just have to ride it out. It should pass quickly. But, in the meantime, I'm not sure what the wormhole will bring us."

"Reclaim restored," the computer said. Just then, a wormhole opened in the center of the room.

Xela clasped her hands together. "Please be Rubi and Gogol. Please be Rubi and Gogol," she chanted.

It was not Rubi and Gogol. Instead, two Earthlings appeared. One was a tall, thin woman dressed in a heavy leather jacket, beige pants and brown boots. Her short cropped hair was pressed flat under a tight leather cap. The other was a male. He wore the same style jacket. In his hand was a map.

The woman looked at Xela and asked, "Od ouy aveh het oordinatesc?"

"What did she say?" Xela asked Autonomou.

"Try again. I've just turned on the room pantawky."

"Do you have the coordinates?" the woman repeated. She slowly looked around. "Where are we, Fred?"

121

"I told you I wasn't sure, Amelia," replied the other Earthling. "Last I knew we were over open ocean outside of New Guinea."

"This is Roma," Xela offered.

"Rome!" said Fred, examining the map. "Impossible, we can't be that far off course."

Amelia looked at Autonomou. "I'm not sure what's going on here, but I am Amelia Earhart, and you have interrupted our journey. Can you send us back, please?"

"Yes, right away. My apologies. But with the space storm still raging, I'm afraid we can't guarantee where you'll end up."

"We'll take that chance," Amelia Earhart said bravely.

"Very well," said Autonomou, as she entered the data. In a few seconds, the two Earthlings were gone.

"Try it again," urged Xela.

"All right," agreed Autonomou. She pressed the reclaim button just as the computer declared, "Planet disconnect. Searching new target."

"Oh no!" screamed Autonomou. "The wormhole lost its lock on Earth. No telling what may come through."

A blast of cold air signaled the new arrival. Autonomou shook her head. "Arms and Xela," she said, "allow me to introduce to you one of the lovely creatures from the planet Mollux."

The creature was huge. Eight feet tall. It had no arms. No legs. Two eyes were set out on tall stalks. And its head, if you could call it that, had a tiny mouth at its tip. It was wet and slimy and gray. It smelled greasy. It looked like a giant slug. Except that it was dressed in a stiff white collar and a fez.

When it spoke, its voice sounded like steam escaping. "This abduction will not go unpunished. I am the Supreme Leader! My troops will . . ."

"Sorry, pal. Wrong number," said Autonomou. She quickly turned back around in her chair and hit reverse. In an instant, the creature was gone. But its smell stayed behind.

"Pew! Remind me to skip that vacation spot," I said.

"Planet connection restored," said the computer. But something was wrong. The golden glow of the crystal was fading.

"The storm has passed," said Autonomou.

"Then we have to try again. Now!" said Xela.

"I'm trying," said Autonomou, "but our power is fading for some reason."

"What's wrong?" Xela was frantic.

"I don't know," said Autonomou. "But if it doesn't work this time, your friends will be Goners 176 and 177." Xela and I looked at each other. We crossed all our fingers and held our breath. Autonomou hit reclaim.

The computer wheezed, coughed, and began to

smoke. Then, nothing. Silence. The glow from the crystal dimmed and then went out.

"No!" screamed Xela. She was so furious, she started pounding on the computer console. "My friends. Give me back my friends!"

"Xela, stop that. It's making the crystal bounce up and down. Keep that up and you'll destroy it!" said Autonomou.

Xela stopped pounding. "I'm sorry," she apologized.

"No. It's all right," I said. "Look!"

The crystal had begun to sparkle. And shimmer. Its glow was so bright we had to shield our eyes.

Autonomou smiled. "Looks like we're back in business."

# 26

## Rubidoux

The basketball ritual went on for another twenty minutes. Once I figured out that I was supposed to put the ball into only one of the hoops, I was unstoppable. I was bigger and faster than the Earthlings. Add to that a little mind reading, and you can imagine how things went. By the time it was over, they wanted me as their leader.

"You're number one, dude!" shouted one of the players.

"I have to admit, you rule," Red smiled. He grabbed my hand and pumped my arm. "Welcome to the team," he said. Then, he turned to face the rest of the humans and yelled, "We are going to kick some serious butt this year!" The reference to violent behavior really seemed to get them going. They began to close in around me, chanting "Ru-bee! Ru-bee! Ru-bee!"

"Break it up. Break it up," Coach Struthers demanded as he forced his way through the butt kickers. "Kid, you're in. You're on the team. Congratulations. Stay after class so we can get all the information we need and get you a practice uniform."

"But . . ."

"Don't thank me, son. Just make sure you keep up those grades." The coach leaned in very close to my face. "If you have any trouble with grades, you come see me first, got it?"

"Yes, but . . ."

"That's all."

"I can't stay."

The coach's face fell. "What do you mean?"

"I mean, I have to go somewhere now."

"Oh. Well, come see us tomorrow. We'll take care of everything then. The coach turned away, ran toward the doors, and yelled, "Dismissed. Hit the showers, guys."

He was too far away to hear me say, "I hope to be back on Roma by then."

Rebecca was waiting for me across the gym. She saw me and waved. I grabbed my hat and trotted over.

"Were you playing basketball?"

"Playing? I thought I was part of some kind of ritual."

"You could say that," she said. "So, where's your friend?"

"Good question. I thought he'd be back by now."

"We'll meet him out front." Rebecca started to leave the gym. "Come on."

I wasn't sure I should leave. "But, wait," I called. She tossed her hair back as she turned to look at me. Her eyelids fluttered. She was smiling. "Let's go," she said sweetly. I couldn't resist. She'd won me over. This talent, combined with the ability to talk nonstop, would definitely make her a good diplomat. I wondered what she would think of DUH.

I walked through the crowded halls with Rebecca. I was watching for Gogol, but couldn't find him. I was distracted by humans pointing at me and whispering my name. "Why is everyone looking at me?" I asked Rebecca.

"Because you're with me and you're, like, cool," Rebecca said cheerfully. She seemed really happy. We stopped at her locker. She made a few quick wrist movements on a dial. Then it opened. "Rebecca, why do you keep things locked in here?" I asked.

"What? You're kidding right? Like they don't have crime in Roma?"

"Actually, they don't."

"Well, it's different here. I have to keep this stuff locked up or it will just walk away, if you know what I mean."

I was trying to imagine the locker stuff getting up and walking away. "Sure," I said, completely unsure, "I get it."

Rebecca slammed the locker door shut. "We're out of here," she said as she put on her jacket and lifted a heavy pouch. Then she headed for the door, along with hundreds of other humans. I still didn't see Gogol. I was hoping he would be outside. The outdoor air was cool, crisp, and moist. There was a lot of tall, colorful plant life lining a wide strip of pavement out front. Personal transport devices zoomed back and forth. Smoke trails followed each one. They were apparently burning something to get energy. Talk about primitive. Many of the devices were stopped and smoking in place. Some of the Earthlings jumped into them. Others just walked or rolled away. They obviously knew better.

"Oh, no!" Rebecca cried.

"What's the matter?" I asked.

"I totally forgot. I can't go with you guys to the golden arches today. I'm really sorry," she said, looking sad.

"According to Gogol, there is nothing more important than visiting the arches at least once a day."

"I totally agree. Like I grabbed breakfast there.

It's just that I have to go to the mall with my mom. She's picking me up."

"Quite a strong woman," I remarked.

Rebecca let out a small laugh. She looked down. I looked down, too. She was slowly grinding the toe of her shoe into the ground. She raised her eyes and looked into mine. "You're cute," she said shyly.

This felt like it must be an Earthling compliment. I could see she was waiting for a response. Using my best diplomatic skills, I came up with, "You're cute too, Rebecca." Then I added, "I'm going to miss you."

"Hey, I'll see you tomorrow. Unless you hop a plane back to Roma or something. Here," she said, scribbling on a piece of paper. "Take this."

Two toots of a signal horn from one of the vehicles commanded our attention.

"That's my mom," she said.

"Which transport is she in?" I asked, looking past her.

"It's that old red-and-white boxy one. Mom says it's a classic."

It was obvious which one she meant. It was very different from the other transports that were lined up. I decided to take a chance. "A '57 Chevy?" I asked.

Rebecca was surprised. "Very good," she said. I didn't want to tell her I knew where her keys were.

Rebecca smiled, looked deep into my eyes one

more time, and said, "Give me a call." Then she turned and walked away. I looked at the paper Rebecca had given me. All that was on it was a series of numbers. I yelled after her, "What's a call?"

She didn't answer. She just looked back at me, shook her long blond hair, and giggled. I'd never heard a laugh quite like it, even with all the life forms on Roma. It was sweet. Gentle. I suddenly felt a bit lightheaded. Maybe Earthlings weren't so hopeless after all. Too bad this planet had been declared off limits. I'd sign up for a mission here any time.

As I watched Rebecca walk away, my warm, tingly feeling seemed to grow stronger and stronger. I felt like I was walking on air! I looked down at my feet to see if I was floating. I wasn't floating! I was disappearing! Roma, here I come!

"If you're looking for your pal, I heard old man Moore has him in the office," croaked a voice. It was Red. "And they're calling the cops!" he added. Red stared at me as I began to dematerialize. His jaw dropped. "Geez, what's going on?"

I just smiled. "Tell Rebecca I hopped a plane to Roma," I said. The last thing I saw were Red's eyes rolling back in his head and his knobby discs buckling as he fainted dead away.

# 27

## Rubidoux

As the exit for the Earth-to-Roma Wormhole Express opened up, I could hear Arms shouting, "We've done it!" And sure enough. There I was. Rematerializing from the top down, right in front of Xela!

"Rubi!" she screamed. "I can't believe it! You're back! You're back!" Then she threw her arms around me. "I was so scared."

"I'm okay," I assured her. "I knew I could count on you two."

"Well, sort of. Rubi, this is Doctor Autonomou," said Arms, pointing to a huge creature who sat at the computer console. "She's the one who did it."

Autonomou came over and patted me on the arm. She didn't know me, but her eyes were filled with tears. The girls must have been telling her about me. "You are one very lucky life form," said the doctor. "I am very happy that . . ."

"Wait!" screamed Xela. "Rubi. Why are you here alone? Where's Gogol?"

"He isn't here?" I said, looking around in a panic. "Then he's in deep trouble."

# 28

## Gogol

Mr. Moore swiveled back in his office chair. "Okay, I'm asking you for the third and last time. What school are you from?"

"DUH," I told him once again. "Diplomatic Universal Headquarters."

Mr. Moore ran his large hands over his hairless head, then rubbed his eyes. "Yes, yes, yes. Located in the city of Roma, right?"

"It's not a city. It's a small planet. Actually, a planetoid." Mr. Moore had suggested that honesty would be the best policy. And I agreed. But the more I told the truth, the worse things seemed to get.

I looked up to see a female with hair so white it was almost blue step into the room. "Sorry to interrupt, Mr. Moore, but there is no listing for a school called 'DUH' in a town named 'Roma.' Young man," she said, looking at me sternly, "are you sending us on a wild goose chase?"

I was speechless. What kind of question was that? I struggled for the right words. Then carefully and politely I suggested, "Only if you'd like to go." Blue Hair looked away and shook her head in disappointment.

"You can't find it because Roma is not on this planet," I explained.

"Are you on this planet, young man?" asked Blue Hair in a soft voice.

"Never mind that, Mrs. Morelli," said the principal. "I've already called the school psychologist. Why don't you keep an eye out for her?"

*How horrible,* I thought. *What a cruel command!*

"Yes, sir. Call me if you need anything else."

"Thank you, I will," he said. Mr. Moore stood up, came around to the front of his desk, and sat down directly in front of me.

I looked up and gave him my sweetest smile. "Can I go now?"

"Not until we find out what's going on here, son. Trespassing is serious business."

"But I had a pass."

"Right. A false one," Mr. Moore said. He pulled

the wrinkled pink slip from his shirt pocket and pushed it at me. "Where did you get this, anyway?"

"Rebecca gave it to me," I assured him.

"Rebecca? We have several Rebeccas here," snapped Mr. Moore. "Rebecca James? Rebecca Watson? Becky Lightfoot? Any of those ring a bell?"

"She was definitely not a bell ringer," I replied.

Mr. Moore got up and went back behind his desk. "Okay, kid. You leave me no choice. I'm going to have to call your parents."

"I'm afraid they are out of voice range."

"Well, then," said Mr. Moore. "We'll just use the phone, now won't we?" Then sharply, he added, "What's the number?"

I wanted to help him, but I believe in being honest. "I don't know what you mean," I said.

"This is a telephone. I'm going to use it to call your parents. I do that by entering seven numbers. Then, like magic, their phone rings and we talk."

"Oh, I see. Thank you."

"So what's their phone number?"

"They don't have a phone," I replied.

B-r-r-r-ing! The unit Mr. Moore held in this hand suddenly rang. "Principal Moore here," he answered. "Hello. Yes, Sergeant. Yes, I did. Thank you. Uh-huh. Good-bye."

Mr. Moore gave me a tight, little smile. "Well, son. That was Sergeant Cooper down at the station.

The police will be here in a few minutes. Maybe you'll tell them what's going on." Then he sat back in his chair, smiled at me, and seemed to relax. "While we're waiting, I want to show you something. See this?" Mr. Moore pointed to a poster on his wall. It was filled with big, blocky letters. The letter *b* seemed to be particularly well represented. "All students at McClean have to live up to certain standards. And it boils down to these five simple things. Why don't you go ahead and read them to me?"

"Be Honest. Be Fair. Be Smart. Be Quick. Be Clean. Beat Central." I was confused. "But that's six."

Mr. Moore's smile faded. "The last one's a joke. Central High is our crosstown rival."

"You must beat them?" I asked.

"Regularly, or school morale goes to zero."

I was so disappointed. Here was more evidence that Earthlings enjoy violence.

"Mr. Moore?" a voice called from the doorway.

"Rita! Come right in," replied Principal Moore. A slight, dark-haired woman in a red, patterned dress entered the room. "Here's your subject. Calls himself Gogol. No last name."

"Hello." The woman looked at me as if she were trying to read my thoughts. "I'm Dr. Rita Lu, the school psychologist."

"Hello," I replied. "Did the human with blue hair

see you?" I was hoping she did. I'd hate to think Mrs. Morelli was walking around without an eye.

Mr. Moore shook his head. "Well, I'll leave you two alone. Don't take too long. Officer Kidder is on his way over."

"Oh, that serious, huh? Okay, we'll just have a little chat," she said as Mr. Moore left the room. Dr. Rita Lu turned to me and smiled. "So. Comfy? Just relax. I'm sure you're a little tense. Can I get you something to drink?"

"No, but I would like a spongy cream-filled cake."

Dr. Lu pursed her lips. "Maybe later. Gogol, let me ask you something. Do you know why you are here?"

"To try and solve the mystery of my origin," I answered.

"Is that why you were pulling all the books off the shelves in the library?" Dr. Lu asked. "I see you kept one." I looked down and to my surprise saw that I was still holding the book named *Thomas Jefferson.*

"I want to learn all I can about Earth. I'm hoping that will help me figure out why I look different from every other creature on my planet."

"We all look a little different," Dr. Lu said slowly. "You seem perfectly normal."

"No. I am smooth-skinned. Everyone else is reptilian," I declared. The doctor was quiet for several seconds. She tilted her head and blinked her eyes rapidly.

"Gogol," she said gently. "Am I a reptile?"

Loud voices from the next room interrupted the conversation. I was glad I didn't have to answer such a silly question. This Earthling was obviously very confused about who she was. Both Dr. Lu and I got up and moved to the door to see what was going on.

The outer office was in turmoil. "All right, son, calm down!" Mrs. Morelli was saying. A student was babbling and making strange, whimpering noises. Several adults were huddled around him.

"Just tell us what happened," pleaded Mr. Moore.

The boy's voice trembled. "He . . . it, I don't know . . . it vanished! I saw it . . . but, it can't be. The new kid . . . I, I, I don't know . . ."

"What new kid?"

"Vanished? Who?"

"The alien!" the boy cried. "His friend . . . is he still here? You've got to watch out!"

"All right, break it up." A man in a blue uniform with a hat even stranger than Rubi's entered the office. The humans moved to greet him and I got a look at the boy who was talking. It was the one called Red.

Mr. Moore extended his hand. "Officer Kidder, thanks for coming. We've got a situation here . . ."

"Ahhhh!" screamed Red. He was staring straight at me. His eyes were wide with fear. "There he is!

There he is! He's an alien! Don't zap me, space-man! Please!"

Dr. Rita Lu began taking notes. "Well, this is turning out to be an interesting day."

"Kid, get a grip," demanded Officer Kidder. Red covered his eyes and moaned. Officer Kidder looked at me. "Is this the one you called me about?"

"Yes," said Moore. "He's been very disruptive and won't answer our questions."

I started to explain, but stopped suddenly as a strange, tingling sensation swept over me. I knew what it meant. I was on my way back to Roma!

"Don't worry, Joe," the officer said to Mr. Moore. "I'll give him the third degree." I didn't like the sound of that. Thank Erin I was decomposing!

"I told you! I told you!" Red screamed. "Look, he's disappearing! Let me out of here! Ahhhh!" Red tumbled over several chairs and raced down the hall.

The policeman watched as I slowly faded away. "Hey, you!" he shouted. "I didn't say you could go."

Officer Kidder lunged forward to seize me, but it was too late. All he came up with was an armful of air. Everyone else just stared in stunned silence as I disappeared one molecule at a time. The last thing I heard as I headed home through the wormhole was Mrs. Morelli asking, "Is it chilly in here, or is it just me?"

Rubidoux

"Do you have him locked in?" I asked as I paced the room.

"There's no telling for sure, Rubi. All I know is that we have locked onto some kind of life form," Autonomou said in a strained voice. It was obvious it had been a long night. She was clearly tired.

"I hope it's not another space slug," groaned Xela.

"No, this is definitely a life form from Earth," said Autonomou. The computer whined and rattled. Then it cheerfully announced, "Wormhole connection weak. Connection will be terminated in seven seconds."

"Oh no!" cried Autonomou. "It can't be."

"Five . . ."

"What's happening?" Arms screamed.

"Do something!" yelled Xela at the same time.

"Four . . ."

"I'm trying," bellowed Autonomou. Suddenly, the golden glow of the crystal flashed across the console as its circuits cloned themselves.

"Three . . ."

"Excellent! We just got a power boost from the crystal!" the doctor exclaimed.

"Please be enough to bring Gogol home," pleaded Arms as she crossed all of her fingers.

"Two . . ."

Suddenly, a blast of cold air filled the room. "It's Gogol! It's Gogol!" I screamed.

"With luck," said Autonomou.

"One . . ."

A stunned Gogol slid out of the wormhole and onto the floor of Autonomou's lab, headfirst. A nanosecond later the passage slammed shut. The room fell quiet.

"Wormhole termination successful," the computer said happily. "Have a nice day!"

Gogol lay motionless, facedown on the floor.

"Gogol?" I asked.

"I can't look," said Arms. "Is he all there?"

Gogol looked up. There was a smile from ear to ear on that smooth-skinned face of his. Funny, I thought, his looks no longer seemed odd to me. "I'm fine," Gogol said.

The room erupted in shouts of joy. Xela, Arms, and I were hooting and hollering, jumping up and down.

"That was amazing!" said Xela. "Gogol, meet Dr. Autonomou. She's the genius who brought you home!"

Even I gave Gogol a hug. "I wasn't sure you'd make it, pal."

"I wasn't too sure either," said Gogol. "They nearly had me locked up."

Autonomou was strangely quiet. She moved to the spot where Gogol had been kicked out of the wormhole and bent to pick something up. Then she gasped!

"What's wrong?" asked Arms.

Autonomou was deathly pale, as if she'd had a sudden shock. In her hand was a book. "Wh-wh-where did you get this?" she sputtered.

Gogol shrugged. "In the school library."

"Doctor, are you okay?" Arms asked as she came over to help Autonomou to a chair. "Why get all excited about some old book?"

Autonomou's eyes were wide. "This is not just any book. This is a book about Thomas Jefferson!"

"So?" I said.

"Don't you see?" asked Autonomou, pointing to the picture on the cover. "He's *one* of them. He's a GONER!"

## Think the Kids from DUH
## Are the Coolest in the Galaxy?
### Read More About Them in
# GONERS #2: THE HUNT IS ON

## Rubidoux

"Goner? What's a Goner?" I cried. But it was no use. The huge green creature with scruffy orange hair was too busy hopping up and down in delight to answer. Her name was Dr. Autonomou and she was 476 years old. But right now she was acting more like she was two.

"I can't believe it! A Goner! We found a Goner!" Autonomou squealed. Her eyes, perched at the ends of two stalks, were open wide. She was staring at a book she held tightly in her massive hands. The whole lab shook as she jumped. "It's him! Ha, ha! It's him!"

We were all staring at Dr. Autonomou in disbelief. I leaned over to Arms, Xela, and Gogol, my friends and fellow students at Diplomatic Universal Headquarters, and whispered, "What's going on?"

"I'm not sure, Rubi," said Gogol. The furry bars above his eyes were arched up high. "All I know is that I accidentally brought that book back with me through the wormhole . . ."

"And as soon as Autonomou saw it, she grabbed it and went crazy," said Arms. Two of her arms shrugged. The other two rested on her waist.

"I think I know what's happening," said Xela, her large yellow eyes gleaming. "See, while you and Gogol were taking your unscheduled field trip to Planet RU1:2 . . ."

"Better known as Earth," piped up Arms.

"Arms and I were here . . ."

"Sick with worry."

"Learning about the mystery of this secret lab."

"And the Goners?" I asked again. "Who, or what, are they?"

"Oh, please forgive me," Autonomou said. "I can explain." She'd finally stopped bouncing, which was fine with me. It was getting pretty annoying. On my home planet of Douxwhop we bop, but we make it a point never to hop. "For a moment I forgot there's no way anyone at DUH would have taught you about the Goners. I've lived with the secret for so long. So—what do you see when you look at the cover of this book?"

"I see a life form that looks a lot like me," answered Gogol.

"You wouldn't have believed it, girls," I said. "There's a whole planet crawling with Gogol look-alikes. Two eyes, two ears, straight hair, smooth skin. What's the universe coming to?"

"Very funny," said Gogol.

"Excuse me, I thought we were talking about Goners," Autonomou barked.

"Okay," said Arms. "So we're looking at a picture of an Earthling called Thomas Jefferson. That's nice."

"Aha!" chirped Autonomou. "That's where you're wrong. Look at the eyes. And the hair. This isn't an Earthling at all. This is mission specialist Noss-Mott. He was one of the first to go to Earth. A dear friend of mine. A life form from Planet Grinz. Covered with reddish blond fur and graced with deep smiling eyes. When mission specialists take the form of Earthlings, certain characteristics survive the transformation. That's how I know this is him. I can see it in the eyes."

Gogol and I looked at each other, then at Arms and Xela. "But what's a Goner?" pleaded Gogol.

Arms Akimbo ran two of her hands across her head while cracking her other twelve fingers. Talk about a racket! "You missed a lot when you were on Planet RU1:2," she said.

"Like for starters," continued Xela, "Dr. Autonomou here, the one who got you back, is the *same* Autonomou you and I read about in those ancient books we found in the library, Rubi."

My tentacles began to stir as I searched my memory banks. Then it came to me. "Wormhole theory? *That* Dr. Autonomou?"

"Exactly," said Xela.

"But that Dr. Autonomou has been dead for years."

Autonomou cleared her throat. "In the words of a great Earthling, 'Reports of my death have been greatly exaggerated.' " We all looked at her with blank expressions. "Sorry," she said with a smile. "I forgot. You wouldn't know. Mark Twain, Philadelphia, Planet Earth, 1897."

Dead or alive, brilliant scientist or not, this Autonomou seemed a little kooky. I shook my head and looked at Xela for help. "Okay, let's just say this *is* Dr. Autonomou. So what?"

"So," Xela said, "two hundred years ago, Autonomou sent 175 mission specialists to Earth to teach the locals the ways of peace. But something went wrong. All contact was lost. The High Council of the Planetary Union decided Earth's violent ways were to blame."

"So they smashed the wormhole connection," chimed in Arms.

"I tried to tell them a *faulty* wormhole connection was to blame, but no one would listen to me," sighed Autonomou.

Xela hung her head. "The mission specialists were left behind."

I was beginning to get the picture. "They're Goners?"

"All 175 of them," confirmed Arms. "Ever since then, Autonomou's been working in secret to reconnect the wormhole to Earth so she can bring them back."

"Well, it's working!" I nearly shouted. "Gogol and I are living proof!"

Autonomou looked very serious. Almost sad. She shook her head. "We were lucky this time. Very lucky. Until tonight the only things I've succeeded in bringing back are the things you see on the shelves. Single socks, keys, loose change, puzzle pieces . . . the hat on your head."

"Oh, sorry," I said. I took the brown felt fedora off and put it back where I'd found it. "I forgot I was wearing it."

Autonomou chuckled. "That's all right. But my point is that this system is still experimental. It will take years of testing to perfect it."

"Years?" exclaimed Gogol. "Life forms are stranded down there! The system *works*."

"You *have* to try and bring them back," agreed Xela.

"And I will," said Autonomou. "In time."

"We can help," offered Gogol. "Rubi and I know all about Earth. And no one is a better computer assistant than Arms. You can send us and we can . . ."

"No!" roared Autonomou. "I'm not risking another life. When it's time, I'll go. But that won't be for . . ."

Xela quietly went over to the doctor and took her hand. Looking up into her eyes, Xela said calmly, "Doctor, that time is now."

Autonomou turned to gaze at the computer screen. She had a faraway look in her eyes, as if some distant goal were coming into focus. For several seconds there was complete and absolute silence. Then, slowly, she said, "I have been working alone and in secret for so many years that I was actually beginning to think the High Council was right. Maybe the Goners were . . ." Autonomou turned her head away, too choked up to continue. Then shaking off the thought, she held up the Thomas Jefferson book and smiled in triumph. "But your discovery changes everything. I finally have proof that *I* was right! I must try to make contact. I'll start with Noss-Mott. There are, of course, modifications to make, and I . . ."

Suddenly, an alarm went off! I practically jumped out of my skin! After everything we'd been through that night, I was more than a little edgy. Autonomou began to laugh. "So sorry! That's just my dawn alarm letting me know the suns will be up soon."

"It's suns up?" cried Xela. "We've got to get back to DUH or we'll be toast."

"Right," Gogol said, "but first I have something to say to Doctor Autonomou. I just want to thank you for getting Rubi and me back from Earth."

"Sorry for the trouble," I added, dropping my most dazzling smile on her.

"Don't give it a thought. Your adventurous spirit has pushed my project far ahead. I want you to get some sleep tonight—then come back tomorrow after school. You can help me prepare for my journey to Earth by teaching me everything you learned about RU1:2."

"Can we all come?" asked Arms.

Autonomou considered the question as she looked at us one by one. "Yes," she said with a grin. "All of you come back. We have a lot of work ahead of us."

"Roma-rama!" shouted Arms.

# THINGS CAN'T GET ANY EERIER
## ...OR CAN THEY?

## Don't miss a single book!

**#1: Return to Foreverware**  by Mike Ford
79774-7/$.99 US/$.99 Can

**#2: Bureau of Lost**  by John Peel
79775-5/$3.99 US/$4.99 Can

**#3: The Eerie Triangle**  by Mike Ford
79776-3/$3.99 US/$4.99 Can

**#4: Simon and Marshall's
Excellent Adventure**  by John Peel
79777-1/$3.99 US/$4.99 Can

**#5: Have Yourself
an Eerie Little Christmas**  by Mike Ford
79781-X/$3.99 US/$4.99 Can

**#6: Fountain of Weird**  by Sherry Shahan
79782-8/$3.99 US/$4.99 Can

**#7: Attack of the
Two-Ton Tomatoes**  by Mike Ford
79783-6/$3.99 US/$4.99 Can

Buy these books at your local bookstore or use this coupon for ordering:
Mail to: Avon Books, Dept BP, Box 767, Rte 2, Dresden, TN 38225          G
Please send me the book(s) I have checked above.
❑ My check or money order—no cash or CODs please—for $_____is enclosed (please
add $1.50 per order to cover postage and handling—Canadian residents add 7% GST). U.S.
residents make checks payable to Avon Books; Canada residents make checks payable to
Hearst Book Group of Canada.
❑ Charge my VISA/MC Acct#_____Exp Date_____
Minimum credit card order is two books or $7.50 (please add postage and handling
charge of $1.50 per order—Canadian residents add 7% GST). For faster service, call
1-800-762-0779. Prices and numbers are subject to change without notice. Please allow six to
eight weeks for delivery.
Name_____
Address_____
City_____State/Zip_____
Telephone No._____                              EI 1097

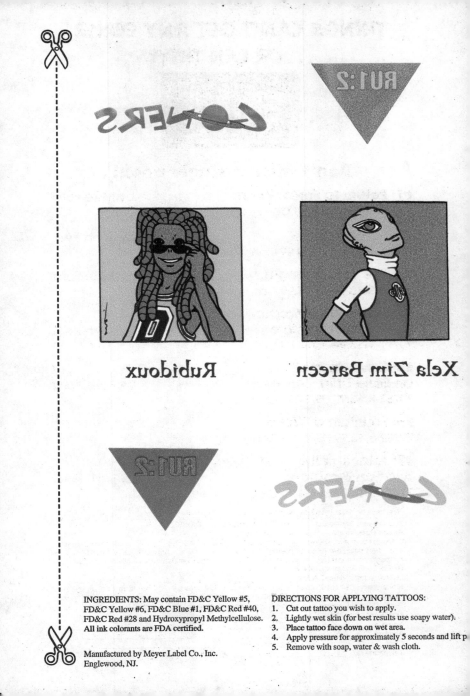

Rubidoux

Xela Zim Bareen

INGREDIENTS: May contain FD&C Yellow #5,
FD&C Yellow #6, FD&C Blue #1, FD&C Red #40,
FD&C Red #28 and Hydroxypropyl Methylcellulose.
All ink colorants are FDA certified.

Manufactured by Meyer Label Co., Inc.
Englewood, NJ.

DIRECTIONS FOR APPLYING TATTOOS:
1. Cut out tattoo you wish to apply.
2. Lightly wet skin (for best results use soapy water).
3. Place tattoo face down on wet area.
4. Apply pressure for approximately 5 seconds and lift p
5. Remove with soap, water & wash cloth.